ALL I WANT

HOLIDAY HEARTS

SUSAN SCOTT SHELLEY

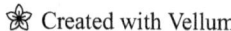 Created with Vellum

CHAPTER ONE

Dodging November wind and rain, Damon Kallis rushed through the parking lot and into Kallis Toy Factory. He was late. Really late. How he'd managed to screw up his own schedule, he didn't know. But he had. And this wasn't the first time since the whole ugly ordeal had begun.

Two meetings, one with his lawyer and the other with a vendor, had overlapped. And now, he was ridiculously late to his own staff meeting.

A lousy start to the week.

He strode through the halls, nodding hello and exchanging greetings. When he reached the meeting room, his dad stood at the front, bringing the meeting to a close with one of his classic jokes.

Uh oh.

It didn't look good when the VP was a no-show, and the company's president had to take over. He waited until the room had emptied and then joined his dad. "I'm sorry. Thanks for covering for me."

His dad clapped him on the shoulder and sighed heavily. "A little notice that you weren't going to make it would've been nice, but I had it covered. Meeting with the lawyers was more important anyway. How did it go with Myers?"

"No lawsuits have been filed yet." He rubbed his hands over his face and sighed. "He's optimistic there won't be, since no one's reported any injuries, and we sent out the recall as soon as the first issue happened."

What a disaster that had been. Exploding ion batteries. A total firetrap. It didn't get much worse than that for a toy manufacturer. And on his brainchild, too. He'd been so proud of the teddy bear that synced with parents' cell phones so they could input sentences into the voice box and virtually chat with their children. They'd sold faster than the company could make them.

With six weeks until Christmas, the timing couldn't have been worse. Damon shook his head. "We're going to take a bigger hit than we'd thought. I don't even want to think about layoffs."

His parents went out of their way to make the company a family atmosphere, hiring local and keeping employees long-term. Kallis Toys was well-loved in the Buffalo suburb of Holiday, New York, and Damon didn't want to see anything happen that would change that, or hurt his employees.

"We haven't had any layoffs in the nearly thirty years that we've owned this company, and we're not starting now. We won't let it come to that." His dad nodded, determined, and Damon chose to believe him. They'd do whatever they needed to keep every employee with them. "But it would be helpful if you could get yourself here on time. I'm not used to running your department meeting. If this was a one-time thing, I'd understand, but you were late to the board meeting last week, and it doesn't look right when my VP, who also happens to be my son, breezes in as though the rules don't apply to him."

Oh hell.

It was like all his years of hard work and dedication didn't matter just because he'd screwed up his schedule a handful of times over the last month.

"I'm sorry. You know how much I care. The screw-ups with my schedule are temporary."

His dad's mouth tightened into a frown. "Let me catch you up, in case your team mentions it. I heard from the contractor this morning. Both the plumbing and electric work were completed. But I think we'll put a hold on the rest of the renovations for now until we see what happens in the aftermath of the recall."

"Good plan." Even though that meant staying in his temporary office a while longer. The renovations to his floor had started due to major damage from a leaking pipe. He and his team were in an unused space, cramped quarters, on a different floor. He still had his own office, but it wasn't the same as the familiar room he'd occupied for years.

His phone buzzed with texts and emails. He scrolled

through them and swore. "I have to go, Dad. I double-booked my afternoon."

That pinched expression returned. "Why haven't you hired a new assistant yet? It's been more than a month since Charlotte retired."

"I don't need one." The truth was, he didn't want one. Didn't want someone poking into things, being in his space, having so much access to his life. His last assistant had been with the company for twenty years. She'd been more like an aunt than an employee, always dispensing advice and completely trustworthy. He wasn't going to find that by bringing on someone new.

His own trust issues prevented it. "Look, I'm managing."

"Not managing too well, as far as I can see. Maybe I should hire one for you."

Uh oh. "Maybe we shouldn't pour money into a new hire until we see what develops from the recall."

"Son, I don't make it a point to stick my nose into your personal business, but when it spills over into affecting the company, I can't keep quiet. Hire that assistant or I will."

"I'll handle it." He had to, somehow.

His dad didn't speak during the walk to the elevator, but then shot him a look over the top of his glasses. "Keep me posted about your interviews."

Which meant he'd be following up.

Mood dark, Damon headed to his office. Aidan and Hunter, his best friends, met him in the hall.

A wide smile beaming across his face, Hunter

clapped Damon on the back. "Ready for lunch? Kira said she'd meet us here in a few minutes."

"I need to put out a fire first." He unlocked the door and stepped inside his office. The guys followed him in and dropped into the guest chairs in front of his desk.

Aidan leaned back, his tall frame almost too big for the chair. "Everything all right?"

"Double-booked a meeting."

"Again?" Hunter huffed out a laugh. "Is that the third or fifth time this month?"

"Not funny." He glared at his friend and opened his laptop and then groaned at his full inbox.

"You need some help?" Hunter's voice was serious, all traces of humor gone. "Just say the word."

Aidan nodded in agreement, and for the first time all morning, Damon's spirits lifted. The three of them had always had each other's backs, ever since meeting in boot camp. Their friendship spanned nearly ten years, cemented by boot camp and then serving in the same unit, and then working together at the toy company. When he'd left the Army, he hadn't been able to let go of his lifelines. So he'd hired them, Hunter in IT and Aidan in HR.

He hated to admit it now, but this was Hunter and Aidan. Maybe they wouldn't give him too much shit. He grimaced. "I, uh, apparently need to hire an assistant."

Aidan raised a single eyebrow and cocked his head to the side. "You'd have one by now if you hadn't found fault with every single candidate out of the twenty you interviewed."

"They weren't right." But who was he kidding? No one would be right.

His friends exchanged glances, and he puffed out his chest, feeling the temptation to snap.

Laughter trickled into the room, followed by his sister Kira and her friend Emily. Kira waved at them and then bent to kiss Hunter. "Emily stopped by for a visit, so I told her to join us for lunch."

Emily greeted them all, and her chocolate brown eyes landed on Damon last. He sat up straighter. Gorgeous, simply gorgeous. She knocked him out. Always had. Soft curves transformed her simple red sweater and blue jeans. Long mahogany-colored hair cascaded over one shoulder. She brushed a strand out of her face, her smooth olive skin glowed, and when she caught Damon's gaze, the smile on her berry-pink lips deepened.

Mouth gone dry, he managed to speak. "Good to see you again."

"You too, Damon."

Heat washed through his chest and his body tightened when she said his name. In all the years that she'd been friends with Kira, they'd never been unattached at the same time.

Until now.

He tried to tell himself he wasn't interested. She wasn't the type of woman for a quick fling, and his heart wouldn't allow him anything more.

Kira sat on the edge of his desk. "So, where are we eating?"

He cleared his throat and had to remind himself that they were talking about lunch and that anyone besides Emily was in the room with him. "You guys decide. I need five minutes to move one of my three o'clock appointments."

"You double-booked yourself again?" His sister leaned over to peer at his calendar. He minimized it, but that left his overflowing inbox in view. Sighing, she shook her head. "Damon. You need help."

"I know, I know. I'm working on it."

"Not fast enough." She stood, and then her eyes gleamed. "I've got it. You need an assistant and Emily needs a job. There. Problem solved."

He raised his gaze. "What?"

At the same time, Emily turned to her. "What?"

"It's perfect. Damon is a mess and Emily is great at organizing." Kira brushed her hands together. "And you don't need to go through a lengthy hiring process because we've all known her forever."

He stood. And caught Hunter smirking and elbowing Aidan in the side. His friends were enjoying his sister's interference. "You can't just…"

But then Emily captured his gaze and she bit her lip, her eyes growing dark with disappointment before turning back to Kira. "Kira, it's okay. I'm sure I'll find something else soon."

"It's been weeks and weeks, and you haven't had any luck. You said you weren't sure about being a reporter anymore. So work here. It'll be great to have you."

"I…" She turned those deep brown eyes back to Damon. "It's up to Damon. But I really am good at organizing."

How could he fight against the mix of uncertainty and hopefulness in her gaze? He needed help, even if he didn't like it, and she needed a job. If he didn't hire her —hire someone—he knew his dad would make good on his threat to take on the hiring process himself. At least this way, he had some control. Although not much, with Kira on a roll.

He pushed down the refusal fighting to break free and tried for a smile. "If you want the job, it's yours."

When she smiled, the room's warmth increased. "I do."

She held her hand out to him, and he clasped it. Electricity shot through him when their palms touched. Her eyes widened—she'd felt it too. He hadn't had that reaction to anyone in ages. He withdrew, slower that he'd planned because his body was overriding his brain's command.

"Welcome to Kallis."

He just hoped he wouldn't regret it.

CHAPTER TWO

Emily dropped her hand to her side. The rush of heat she'd felt when her hand had joined with Damon's remained. He was tall, over six foot, with dark eyes that sparked heat and intensity, and toast brown hair he wore a tad too long flattered his strong face. Positioned behind the desk, he looked powerful with his muscular frame packed into a blue striped button-down shirt and gray pants.

She glanced down at her jeans, boots, and red sweater. By far, the most casual outfit she'd ever worn for an interview. Of course, if she'd had any idea that she'd be sprung into an interview, she would've worn something more appropriate.

But that was Kira. Her best friend had always been that way, ever since they'd met as roommates their freshman year of college. She always meant well, and if there was a chance she could help out in any way, she jumped at it with total enthusiasm.

Emily was grateful. She needed a job, and thanks to her ex, she wasn't having any luck finding one at any of the TV stations in Western New York. But did Damon really want her? He seemed less than enthused.

"Congratulations." Kira hugged her. "Lunch will be a celebration. Why don't we just order from the Greek deli and have it delivered? That way, Emily can get settled more quickly and help Damon get back on track."

Damon shot his sister a dark look and picked up his phone. "Order my usual for me?"

"Done." Kira pulled her toward the door. "Come on, Em. I have a menu in my office."

Aidan rose and joined them. "Emily, you don't happen you have your passport or social security card, do you? I'll need to see one of those and your driver's license."

"I actually do have my passport. I was in Toronto this weekend and didn't take it out of my purse yet." She made the two-hour drive with her sisters a few times a year to visit their Canadian cousins.

"Perfect. I'll grab some paperwork you'll need to fill out. You can do that while we eat."

Hunter hefted himself out of the chair and followed. "After lunch, I'll get you set up in the system, and with a workstation." Then he paused. "Damon, where will she be working? None of the desks on the outer floor are vacant, and there isn't much room to add another."

In the middle of dialing, Damon set the phone down

hard. His brows lowered and he looked annoyed—whether from the continued interruptions to his phone call or the dilemma of where to place her, she wasn't sure. Eventually, he sighed. "I guess putting her on a different floor wouldn't make much sense. It looks like Emily will be sharing with me."

She glanced around the room, and her fingers tightened on her purse strap. Tension rolled off him in waves.

Hunter nodded. "I'll have a desk and computer sent up."

A muscle jumping in his jaw, Damon lifted the phone again. His shirt stretched tight across tense shoulders. "Great."

Emily followed Kira into the hall. "Are you sure about this? Damon doesn't seem too happy."

"He's fine." She waved to Hunter and Aidan. "I'll get your usuals, too."

"Kira…" The discomfort in Emily's stomach grew stronger.

"Okay." She didn't speak until they were alone in the elevator, and traveling back to the Marketing floor. "I'd mentioned that Damon has some trust issues. He'll be fine. He just needs a little time to get used to the idea, that's all."

"All right…" It occurred to her that they hadn't discussed salary or benefits or anything else usually mentioned in an interview. Kallis Toys had a good reputation and the highest employee retention in the state.

Everyone she passed seemed happy. For now, she'd take it no matter what it paid. Bills were piling up.

Lunch was a whirlwind of Greek salad and paperwork—where she had the salary and benefits questions answered and was pleasantly surprised by the company's generosity—followed by helping everyone rearrange Damon's office to accommodate the second desk. Their desks were positioned on opposite sides of the room, facing each other. Kira and Aidan stocked hers with supplies while Hunter showed her how to log on to the company email system and a few tips and tricks for navigating some of the company software.

And then, a blink later, they were gone, and she was left alone with Damon. She sat at her desk, her pen poised over a notepad. "What do you need help with? What did your last assistant do?"

"A lot." But he didn't elaborate. Damon leaned back in his chair. "Why did you leave your last job?"

The interview-type question wasn't unexpected. He had a right to ask and to know. She set down the pen and mirrored his position. "It became a hostile atmosphere."

"Co-workers? Management? Harassment? Something specific?"

She took a deep breath, trying to decide how much to share, then decided to spit out the whole miserable tale. "I worked at Channel 10 and was dating a co-worker. We were working on a big story together, but he took full credit. Our boss didn't believe me when I protested, and my files and emails were somehow deleted from my computer, so I didn't have any proof."

Damon's brows rose and his muttered expletive echoed the frustration Emily still carried.

She continued, playing with her bracelet as she spoke. It had been her grandmother's and she always wore when she needed an extra boost of confidence. She'd worn it a lot since that debacle at the station. "After that, working there became uncomfortable. The boss started acting like she couldn't trust me, giving assignments to him and undercutting me at every turn. I couldn't deal with it anymore. I left a few months ago, but finding a job at another station has been impossible."

His gaze had sharpened and she lifted her chin, trying to get a read on him, but she couldn't. "You think your co-worker deleted the files, don't you?"

"Though it was my personal computer, I'd given him access. We were spending a lot of time together, and it was easier for him to just go to my computer and bring up the material than go through the trouble of sharing. I'd trusted him. And he was the only one besides me with the passwords. I changed them all the time. After that, well—I felt so betrayed. It made me reevaluate a lot of things." But discussing her ex wasn't important. No matter how much the betrayal still stung. "Look, my being a reporter means I'm great at research and fact-checking, and I understand deadlines and pressure. And I really am good at organizing anything from offices to schedules to closets. I think I'll be a good assistant."

"I'm sure. In fact, you're way over-qualified."

Her heart dipped, afraid he'd let her go right then and there.

Instead, he leaned forward and matched her gaze, and the skin around his eyes relaxed. "I understand reevaluating. I've done it more than once myself."

The very air seemed to still, to hush, as they watched each other. Kindreds in pain and heartache and disappointment. "I'm glad you understand."

Then, he seemed to pull back into himself. "We have a lot going on right now. I'm sure you heard about the toy recall. It was all over the news."

She nodded.

"That's taking up a lot of my time. So is redesigning the new version."

"What can I do to help?"

Elbows on the desk, he clasped his hands together, making a steeple out of both index fingers. "We're holding a charity gala in mid-December. The first thing I'd like you to do is take over the preparations. It's a big deal. Members of the Buffalo sports teams will be there, and people pay to mingle with them. At the end of the night, we present a check to the Children's Hospital."

"Whatever you need me to do."

"I'll forward you the information. My former assistant completed a lot of it, but I need things followed up on and double-checked."

She offered him a smile. "I can do that."

"Good. We'll start there." He returned her smile, but it didn't meet his eyes.

They worked for a while without speaking to each other. Damon made phone call after phone call, and his fingers pounded away at his keyboard. She stayed busy with comparing lists for the party and answering responses to the company-wide welcome email Aidan had sent out, announcing her as a new hire. All the while, half of her attention was focused on her new boss. She'd known Damon nearly as long as she'd known Kira, and while he'd been friendly, even flirty, they'd never gotten close.

But now they could.

Nothing was stopping them from exploring the undercurrent of attraction that had charged their interactions over the years.

Nothing but the fact that he was now her boss.

Dating a co-worker hadn't been smart.

Dating her boss had mistake written all over it. In capital letters.

But…

She liked the way the afternoon sun brought out the highlights in his hair. And the way his broad shoulders filled out his shirt. And that he was nice to all the people he interacted with. He was a hard worker, moving from one task to the next with military precision, and his team clearly liked and respected him.

He was pleasant to her, but there was definitely a guard in place. His body language—the stiff movements, the shifting in his chair, the ramrod posture—indicated that he wasn't comfortable with her presence.

At five-thirty, Kira knocked on the door. "Quitting time. My family is very firm about keeping a good work-life balance. How was your first day?"

"It went well." Emily stretched and looked at Damon. Did he think it had gone well?

Damon shut his laptop and stood. "Can you be here tomorrow at eight-thirty? I'll meet you in the break room."

Kira sat on the edge of Emily's desk while she shut down her computer. "We always start with coffee."

"I'll be there." She slipped into her coat and gathered her purse.

Together, the three of them walked to the door, and Damon paused to lock it behind him. He was silent during the elevator ride to the main lobby and then bid them a quick goodnight before heading across the parking lot.

Emily shivered as the cold wind whipped around her and settled deep in her bones. "I know he and I were never close friends, but he wasn't always so closed off."

Kira pulled on a hat and gloves. "The last year has been hard on him. First with his awful ex, and then with the recall. But tonight, he has a hockey game, which means he'll be in a better mood tomorrow. He's always happier after he blows off some steam on the ice. Actually, since Hunter will be at the game too, why don't you come over and keep me company? We'll bake Christmas cookies."

She laughed. "Isn't it a little early? There are still two weeks until Thanksgiving."

"Then we'll bake Thanksgiving cookies. I'm pretty sure I have a cookie cutter in the shape of a turkey."

"If not, we can bake something else."

Being able to hang out more with Kira was a definite plus. But she wasn't sure how she felt yet about working with Damon.

CHAPTER THREE

Butterflies in his stomach weren't a great way to start the day.

Damon hustled from his car to the warmth of the building's lobby. With each step, nervous energy stirred. Not in anticipation of a big meeting or a big hockey game. But because of a petite brunette waiting for him who'd starred in too many of his dreams and every real-life interaction always left him craving more.

He stepped off the elevator and made his way toward the break room. Laughter and conversations wafted out, accompanied by the scent of coffee and baked goods. He recognized Emily's voice among the tumbling words.

His heartbeat quickened. And those butterflies ramped up to tornado-speed.

Both reactions annoyed him. Scared him. Warned him.

Forewarned was forearmed.

Attraction was a distraction.

He couldn't afford any of those.

Not now.

Too much was riding on his shoulders.

"What are you doing lurking in the hallway?" Hunter's voice jolted Damon from his spot outside the doorway.

"Damn it. Don't do that. I didn't hear you coming."

"No kidding." Hunter gave him a wry smile. "You were miles away. What's going on?"

"Nothing. Morning brain. Need coffee."

Hunter slapped him on the shoulder. "Same."

He glanced over his shoulder and spied Aidan heading their way. Even though they'd seen each other earlier in the morning at the running trail, as they did most days a week, they still started their workdays together in the break room.

As Aidan approached, cell phone pressed to his ear, he waved. The nerves swirling in Damon's gut stilled. His two best friends had been by his side for years. They always had each other's backs. They'd help distract him from Emily, not that he'd tell them what was going on there.

Aidan pocketed his phone. "Why are we out here?"

"We were waiting for you." Damon lightly elbowed him in the gut. "Let's go."

Hunter shuffled into the break room, greeting Kira and Emily.

Damon waved for Aidan to go in front of him. Then, inwardly calling himself a coward, he entered the room.

Emily held a large mug decorated with cartoon holiday lights and dancing reindeer. She wore a soft-looking white sweater, a gray skirt, and knee-high black boots. Her long hair fell over her shoulders in dark waves and her red lips parted in a smile when she met his gaze. "Good morning."

"Morning." The word sounded more like a grunt as it passed his suddenly dry mouth and throat.

Kira turned toward him. "I was just telling Emily about how Skye voiced the new commercial we're airing for the holidays, and how Aidan's dog was the star."

"Getting him to sit was impossible after he saw that stuffed animal squirrel." Aidan laughed as he poured decaf coffee into a mug. "You'd think he'd have realized it wasn't the real thing, but no."

Damon helped himself to the regular brew. "He calmed down once we brought out the dog treats."

"Speaking of Skye voicing things," Aidan's smile broadened when he said his fiancée's name, "Emily, I sent you the links to several new hire overview videos. You should see them in your inbox. If not, call me."

"Will do. Thanks." She glanced from Aidan to Damon. "I brought in cookies if you want one. They're from the batch Kira and I baked last night."

The cookies were next to the station of coffee creamers and sugars. Chocolate chip cookies and… was that sugar cookies shaped like *turkeys*? He couldn't stop the smile tugging at his lips. "I recognize that turkey cookie cutter from last Thanksgiving. We had gingerbread turkey cookies then." He selected a sugar cookie and bit off its head.

"What do you think?" Emily watched him with her teeth biting into her bottom lip. The move brought his attention to the plump curve of her lip and the way her gaze held his made him long for something he wouldn't allow himself to have.

"They're fine. Good." He wrapped the rest of the cookie in a napkin and then focused on doctoring his coffee.

"Cookies for breakfast?" Hunter reached over his shoulder and then grabbed two cookies from the plate. "Best day ever. We should make this a regular thing."

"What—the doughnuts, muffins, and bagels we regularly supply aren't enough?" Kidding with his friend was easier than dealing with the return of the swarming butterflies.

Hunter draped his arm over Kira's shoulders. "Nope."

Emily caught Damon's gaze once again. "It's nice that you provide those things for your employees."

"Everyone works hard and we appreciate them." The reminder of hard work had him glancing at his watch. "Ready to go?"

"Sure." She waved at the others and then followed him into the hallway. The thin heels of her boots clicked against the floor as they walked.

Damon imagined that each *click, click* was another lock on his armor snapping shut. By the time they reached his office, every defense had been shored up.

He unlocked the door, slipped his keys into his pocket, and flipped on the lights.

As always, he did a cursory sweep of the room, making sure everything looked to be in place, before stepping inside.

Emily crossed to her desk. She laid her coat on the back of her chair and stowed her purse in a drawer, and then turned on her computer. "What can I do for you today? How does your schedule look?"

"I'm not overbooked today. But I have a ton of emails to wade through."

"Anything that I can help with?"

He set his coffee and the cookie on his desk and then sat. "Explaining it to you will take longer than just doing it myself."

Her brows drew together. "But—"

"I know. It's a vicious cycle. Taking time to teach you will help in the long run, but taking the time now means using time I don't have to spare. Let me get through some of this and then we'll see."

Her mouth opened and closed and then opened again and the hesitation written across her features tugged at something deep within him. "All right. Then I guess I'll jump into those new hire overview videos Aidan sent."

"Good idea."

He locked his attention on his inbox and for the next three hours, he handled issue after issue, passed off what he could to his team, and moved things that he would've forwarded to his old assistant into a folder. He would deal with those after hours, from the comfort of his own apartment and on his own time.

At eleven-thirty, his calendar's reminder alert chimed. He shut down his computer, stood and stretched, and then focused on Emily. They hadn't spoken much during the few hours they'd been together, other than the few interruptions he'd had when members of his team came in. "I have a meeting."

Her pen paused over the paper he'd asked her to proofread once she'd completed watching the videos. "Okay. See you later."

He glanced at the boxes lining the far wall. With everything that had been going on, between the flooding in his regular floor and the chaos of dealing with the fallout of the toy recall, there hadn't been enough time to properly handle those files. Keeping them locked in his temporary office had seemed to be the easiest solution, and now, it was going to bite him. Palming his keys, he took a few steps in her direction. "Why don't you take an early lunch?"

"I'm not hungry yet."

The muscles at the back of his neck tightened as frustration over their forced proximity flared to life. His cautious protectiveness over his files warred with the rational side of his thoughts. He had to trust her, sooner or later. But only one day on the job was far too soon. Even though they'd technically known each other for years, she'd always been Kira's friend and his acquaintance. "Look, it's not personal, but I can't have anyone in here without me."

Her brows drew together as she studied him. "You're serious."

"I am. There's sensitive information in here that I haven't had a chance to handle."

"Oh?"

No way did he want to get into more details yet. Desperate for find something for her to do, he scanned his office and relief filled him as his gaze landed on the shipping label at the top of his to-do pile. He grabbed it and its accompanying box and held them out to Emily. "Could you do an errand for me? I'd like to get this in the mail today."

Eyeing the package, she took it. "Um, sure."

"Why don't you do that now, and then take your lunch hour? My meeting should be finished by one-thirty. I'll text you when it's over."

"Okay," The word, tinged with curiosity, dragged across three syllables, but Emily closed her laptop and then slowly stood. The scent of her floral perfume teased the air, light and delicate and Damon had to step back to stop himself from drawing in another intoxicating lungful.

Having her drive to the post office to mail out a package that wasn't a shipping rush might seem extreme, especially since it could technically wait until their mail carrier arrived, but he was grasping for inspiration. He dragged his gaze to his watch and calculated the drive time to the lawyer's office. "Let me give you my cell number in case something comes up."

She slipped into her coat. "Kira gave it to me last night."

"Oh." The fact that she had it, and he hadn't been aware or the one to hand out the info, made him feel just the slightest bit vulnerable.

"She gave it to me in case I had an issue this morning and she wasn't reachable."

"Right. That was a good idea. I should've thought about that yesterday afternoon." Come to think of it, Aidan had mentioned at the rink last night that he'd given Emily his number and she had the office's main number on some of the new hire materials. Damon had been too distracted with thoughts of Emily and how closely they'd be working together to think about specifics.

"No worries." The smile she shot his way hit in right in the solar plexus.

He sucked in a breath and backed up three more steps. "I'll, ah, lock up behind you."

Emily nodded and retrieved her purse from the bottom drawer of her desk and then picked up the package.

Moments later, she was gone.

Damon raked a hand through his hair and blew out a long breath.

He'd keep Emily at a distance. No matter how she tempted him.

One work week.

Five days.

Forty hours.

Ten thousand and eighty minutes.

Six-hundred-forty thousand and eight-hundred seconds.

Damon tipped back his beer and watched the amber liquid slowly draining from the bottle. No matter how he slice the time, it all added up to the same conclusion: spending time with Emily was dangerous. No matter how hard he tried to keep to himself, to keep his guard up, she said or did something that had pieces of the wall crumbling down.

It was scary as hell.

Sprawled on his couch, he tried to focus on the hockey game playing on his TV. The Bedlam were winning, but he hadn't a clue how they'd score those last two goals. The entire night, his thoughts had been focused on the sexy brunette with the kind eyes.

She made him want things. Things he hadn't wanted in months.

Connection.

Kisses.

Caresses.

Affection.

Stop.

Damn it, she worked for him. And, she was Kira's best friend. And, he wasn't sure that his heart was ready to handle another relationship, romantic or otherwise, just yet. All three of which were very good reasons to keep up his shields.

His call box buzzer sounded, followed by the buzzer ending the hockey game's first period. He heaved himself off the couch and hustled to the buzzer.

"Yeah?"

"Hunter and I are here with pizza." Aidan's deep voice carried through the speaker.

Damon blinked. He'd figured that he wouldn't be seeing his friends tonight. "Come on up."

A glance at the living room and kitchen told him the spaces were neat enough. These were his best friends, after all, they'd seen him at his best and at his worst.

He waited by the door and tugged it open when he heard their voices in the hall. "So, what's with the surprise?"

Hunter entered first, holding a six pack of beer. "We figured you needed us."

"Exactly." Aidan followed, holding two boxes of pizza. The scent of tomato sauce trailed behind him.

"Why?" He shut the door and then trailed after his friends.

"You haven't seemed like yourself this week."

Surprise stopped him in his tracks. "Oh."

"Yep. That right there." With a triumphant gleam, Hunter pointed at Damon's face. "That expression says it all. You're not okay."

Opening his mouth to argue, Damon changed his mind, and snapped it shut. He lifted the pizza box lids.

"Double pepperoni, nice. But this other one…" He glanced at the check marks on the toppings. "Fully loaded? Since when do we drown our pizza in veggies?"

Aidan's lips twitched as he grabbed plates from the cabinet. "There's sausage and pepperoni on that one too."

"Want a beer?" Hunter placed the six pack in the fridge and then plucked three fresh bottles from the fridge door. He set one in front of Damon, then the other two down by the other plates.

"Guys," Half-amused at how at-home his friends were in his space, Damon swung his leg over one of the stools at his breakfast bar. "I'm fine."

A supportive hand on his shoulder accompanied Hunter's words. "Yeah, right. As quiet as you've been all week, we haven't seen you like that, not since the Ursula incident."

"We're a little worried," Aidan affirmed. "I know the toy recall and working on the new prototype have been weighing on you, but that's not anything new. The only new addition that we can think of is Emily."

Hunter's features grew solemn. "She seems great, and we all like her. You know how happy Kira is to have Emily with the company. But, if she's not working out for you…"

"No, she's… fine." Damon gripped his bottle and forced a smile. "Everything is fine. Okay?"

Aidan's brows drew together. He studied Damon for a long moment while Damon tried not to give away any feelings. "It's obviously not fine. We don't want to fight with you, we just want to help."

He knew from experience that they wouldn't budge until he caved. Blowing out a breath, he plucked at the edge of the pizza box. "All right. Adjusting to having her around, so close, all the time hasn't been easy."

"I know sharing your space is hard for you. Hell, even Charlotte didn't share your office when you were back on the regular floor, and she worked with you for ages."

"It's not just that. I mean, yes, it *is* that, but… It's also… lunches, and morning coffee, and her freaking perfume and the way she smiles, and how she…" He stopped talking. Both Hunter and Aidan wore identical expressions of surprise.

"Dude." Hunter grinned and then slapped him on the back. "You like her."

"What is this, middle school?" Discomfort rolled through him and he bit into a slice of the fully loaded pizza. After he swallowed, he set food down and leveled a stare at his best friends. "She's my employee. And that's way too close for comfort."

Aidan raised his hands. "But if you—"

"But nothing. I'm not looking for anything. I don't want anything."

After another long pause, and an exchanged look between his friends, Aidan asked, "Are you trying to convince us? Or yourself?"

The argument he'd been poised to make died. He

couldn't lie to his friends. They knew him too well. A heavy weight settled over the pizza in his stomach. "I'll handle it."

He'd find a way to squash his feelings.

The alternative was too risky to consider.

CHAPTER FOUR

The Monday after Thanksgiving, Emily sat in the break room, waiting for Damon. As was their pattern.

Two weeks had passed since he'd hired her.

Two weeks, and yet, she still didn't have a key to his office, still had nothing to do but plan the charity party that was mostly planned, and Damon still gripped control over his inbox and overbooked his schedule. At least three times a day, she'd make a suggestion about a specific task she could do to help him, but he'd always brush her off. Most days, she sat around waiting for something to do, and it was driving her crazy.

She stirred her coffee, trying to solve the mystery that was Damon. When they were alone, he was quiet and brooding. But when she saw him with Hunter and Aidan, or Kira, or an employee, he was a different person, a normal person. A happier person.

It hurt.

On top of that, she needed the job. And it didn't look

like there'd be anything for her to do after the charity party took place.

Multiple pairs of footsteps echoed in the hall, and then Damon entered the room, flanked as usual by Aidan and Hunter. They greeted her and headed for the coffee pots. She knew that pattern now too. Hunter and Damon drank regular, Aidan chose decaf, and Kira always added peppermint creamer to her cup.

She stood, while Hunter poured an extra coffee that she assumed was for Kira. "Where's Kira this morning?"

"Prepping for her department meeting. They're holding it early today." He smiled and added the sweetened creamer to the cup. "How was your Thanksgiving?"

"Too much food, but a lot of fun with my family." She'd appreciated having the long weekend and lots of time for visits with her cousins and sisters. "How about you? You and Kira hosted at your house, right?"

"Yeah." His smile widened to a grin. "Since Aidan and Skye were in Miami visiting her family, we watched their dog. He followed Damon around the whole time."

"And snatched the turkey right off my plate." Damon shook his head and then turned to Aidan. "You need to teach your dog better table manners. He had his own food in the dish on the floor."

Eyes brimming with laughter, the gentle giant shrugged. "From what your sister said, you're the one who let him sit on your lap when you were at the table.

You share your seat, he thinks you're also going to share your plate."

Damon shook his head again, but he was laughing too. Then he met Emily's gaze, and the merriment faded to something she couldn't name. "Ready to get to work?"

"Sure." She bit back the response that she'd been ready and waiting for more work to do for two weeks. Calling him out in front of his friends wasn't her style, but once they were alone, all bets were off.

They walked side by side to his office. He unlocked the door and turned on the lights and went straight to his desk.

She draped her coat over the back of her chair. Smoothing the soft wool soothed her. "What can I do for you today?"

"In addition to the charity gala, we also need to get things going for the employee holiday party on Christmas Eve. I'll get you the information from last year's party. You can contact the same caterer and see about food options."

More party planning.

Yay.

Not.

Frustration ate away at her patience. She understood that the charity event was a big deal and that the employee event was important, but neither of those things was enough to fill her schedule. "That's not going to take me eight hours. I'm sure you have more going on. What else can I help with?"

His focus was on his computer screen. "I have a conference call with Children's Hospital at nine-thirty tomorrow that's interfering with my meeting with the events coordinator from the Buffalo Bedlam hockey team."

She wasn't surprised. He apparently thought he was a superhuman and could fly to the appointments he'd booked too close together. "You also have your Monday morning staff meeting in fifteen minutes, so while you get ready for that, I can reschedule the appointment for you."

He shook his head. "I'll do it after the meeting."

A sigh heaved out, and she dropped her pad on her desk. She'd had enough. "If you wanted a party planner, you should have just hired one. But you hired an assistant, and from what I've learned, I'm not doing a single thing that your former one used to do for you."

His brows lifted and then his eyes narrowed. "She helped organize the parties."

"Fine. But that isn't all she did. For most of the past two weeks, I've been sitting around, bored. You're not giving me anything to do, and when I ask for things, you send me on errands to get coffee or lunch. I don't mind grabbing those if you're swamped, but you're swamped because you won't let me help with anything."

She took a breath, and his eyes darkened, but she continued, not giving him a chance to speak. "Is it because you're afraid I'm going to screw something up? Or I'm not experienced enough to reschedule a meeting or talk to a lawyer or vendor? If so, it would help a lot if you'd be honest."

He opened his mouth, but she held up her hand. She wasn't finished. Heart pounding, she snapped out the words. "One more thing. My not having a key is becoming a problem. I'm cooling my heels in the break room while I'm waiting for you to arrive or when you go out to a meeting. I get that you don't want me in your office alone... But I look like a slacker when everyone sees me hanging out there so much. Maybe we should just move my desk in there, and set up a little partition around it. That would at least solve the problem with the key."

Raising her voice might not have been the most professional thing to do, but the man was driving her crazy.

He stood, slowly, eyes glittering, and that muscle jumped in his jaw. Bracing his hands on his desk, he opened his mouth. The phone on his desk rang before he uttered a word. His gaze flicked to it, then he swore and snatched it up. "Damon Kallis."

Emily sucked in a breath. Her pulse still raced, and her stomach felt full of needles. Had she really just yelled at him? Maybe it didn't matter. Maybe she'd be better off leaving, and going into party planning—at least she was gaining experience there. A low-grade thud forming at the base of her skull, she retreated to her desk.

Damon set the phone down. "That was the events coordinator at the hotel. They need to finalize the menu and the decorations for the gala. She wants to meet today. I told her you could head over now."

"Fine. I'll get going."

"And when you come back, we're going to have a conversation." His expression hadn't changed. He was still as angry.

But so was she. "It's about time we did."

She grabbed her laptop, purse, and coat then got out of there before she said something she'd end up regretting or getting fired over.

The elevator stopped two floors down, and Kira stepped on. "Hey. Where are you headed?"

"I'm meeting the event planner at the hotel to finalize the menu for the gala."

"Cool. Make sure there's something chocolate for dessert." Her smile faded as she studied Emily's face. Concern creasing her features, she laid her hand on Emily's arm. "What's wrong?"

She'd always confided in her friend, but confided about Damon seemed almost wrong, somehow, like she was overstepping. "Nothing."

"From the look on your face, I know that's not true. What's going on?"

Torn, she took a breath and searched her mind for an excuse. "Nothing for you to worry about."

A single brow rose and then Kira crossed her arms over her chest. "Let me guess… Damon."

"I…"

"I'm right. I can tell."

"Okay, fine. You're right. But I don't want to complain to you. It doesn't seem right."

"We're best friends."

"We're also co-workers. And your brother is my boss."

"Even so, we're friends first and that supersedes anything else. Also, since I suggested that Damon hire you, I feel responsible. I want you to be happy here. What did my brother do?"

Then and there, Emily decided she wouldn't change confiding in Kira, no matter the circumstance. "I hate complaining to you, especially when I need a job so badly. But…" She forced out the words. "Your brother. He can be very difficult to deal with. Very."

"No kidding. He can be impossible. Why? What did he do?"

Emily gave her a rundown of the conversation with Damon and her frustrations. Unloading on Kira hadn't been the plan, but as Kira had said, she'd been the one to push for Emily to have the job in the first place.

When they reached the main lobby, Kira stepped off with her. "I'm sorry. I'll talk to him."

"I don't want to cause problems between you guys. You don't have to say anything. Maybe what I said to him today will be enough."

"Not likely. Damon is as stubborn as they come. But he's also fiercely protective, and he takes care of his friends."

"I'm not his friend. I'm yours." But that didn't account

for the difference in his attitude. She'd seen the friendly way he interacted with her fellow employees. For whatever reason, he just didn't like her. Had she done something in the past to make him dislike her? She didn't think so.

"Hang in there, okay? I promise it will get better. I'll make sure of it." Kira gave her a hug. "I need to get back to my desk. I'll stop by and see you at lunch."

"Deal."

Emily slowly drove to the hotel. Signs of the holiday season were springing up around town. She should have been happy. She loved Christmas, but her day had been nothing but a headache. And now a real one was brewing behind her eyes. Would she want to be friends with Damon? Of course. Had she entertained more than friendly thoughts about him? Absolutely. But with the way he'd been acting, she didn't think he planned on getting to know her better at all.

Two hours later, her mood hadn't improved. The events coordinator had made noises about calling Damon and confirming the menu and decoration selections with him personally. Being undermined hadn't sat well with Emily, but she had held her ground and reminded the woman that Damon had given the task to her. Determination paid off, swaying the coordinator to leave Damon alone, and by the meeting's end, Emily had checked off every item for the party.

She walked into the coffee shop attached to the hotel, groaning as she rolled her knotted shoulders. Being in her old stomping grounds didn't help her tension. The hotel was close to the news station, and she couldn't keep her focus from drifting over to Channel 10's building while she waited in line.

"Emily? It *is* you."

Her muscles tensed. She'd know that voice anywhere. Digging her nails into her palm, she turned. Paul Redmond, her ex, and the lying bastard who'd cast a cloud of suspicion over her ethics stood in front of her, as plastic and polished as ever. "Paul."

"What are you doing here? Don't tell me you're back at the station. I would've heard about that."

Of course, he would have heard. Because he was so far up the station manager's ass… "Nope. I'm not back at the station."

She turned back to face the counter, pulled her phone from her purse and checked to see if she had any messages. If she ignored him long enough, maybe he'd go away.

Still, he hovered. "Really, what are you doing here?"

Tucking her phone away, she faced him again. "Why? Are you worried I might have found a way to prove that you deleted my files from my computer?"

He blanched and stepped back. "How—I mean, what?"

Letting him worry felt wonderful.

"Look, Em." His throat worked for a second, and his eyes darted around the shop. "You know how cut-throat this business is. No hard feelings, right?"

"No hard feelings?" She gaped at him, and fought to control the level of her voice. "You lied to our boss, made her doubt that she could trust me, and made the work environment hell. But I guess it's for the best. I saw your true colors. So really, I should thank you."

His hand moved toward his perfect hair and then fell to his side. "Where are you working now?"

"Not with you, so that must mean I'm moving up in the world." She stepped up to the counter and ordered a gingerbread latte.

The cashier beamed a smile when Emily dropped a five dollar bill into the tip jar. "Thanks! Don't forget to enter our giveaway. Drop your business card in the box at the end of the counter while you wait for your coffee. You can win coffee and breakfast treats for your entire office."

"Oh, sure. Thanks." Maybe the coffee and treats would win over Damon… She tugged a business card from her wallet. Before she could drop it in the box, Paul plucked it from her hand.

"You're working for Kallis Toys?"

She snatched the card and stuffed it into her coat pocket. Forget the giveaway. She just needed to get away. "Goodbye, Paul."

"Executive Assistant to the VP?"

Huffing out a sigh, she moved further away from him. The barista was working fast, and her latte order was next in line to be filled.

Paul followed her as though she hadn't just told him to kiss off. "You're bound to have information on the toy recall. Last I heard, it cost the company a huge chunk of change. Have there been any lawsuits? Will there be any layoffs?"

Like she'd tell him even if she knew. "Get lost."

"Come on. I only got in one question at the press conference they held last month, and that Damon guy bit my head off."

She smirked and stepped around him, willing the barista to pour the coffee orders faster. "Good for Damon."

He ignored her statement. "He mentioned they were working on a second-generation model that would address all the issues. How's that coming? How close are they to releasing it? This is exactly the scoop I need. I've been searching for information, but nothing's turned up yet. Kallis is guarding it closely."

Finally, her latte was ready. She grabbed it from the counter, then turned to face him. "After what you did to me, do you really think I'd tell you anything?"

His eyes narrowed, and his nostrils flared. "You—"

"Let me save you from guessing. The answer is no. You're a sorry excuse for a reporter, stepping on and using everyone else to push yourself to the top. What you did to me sickens me. And if I had any pull at Kallis —which I *don't*—I'd be sure to send exclusives to anyone other than you." She pushed through the door and out into the cold. Her temples throbbed, and pain tightened into a band around her head. She shouldn't have stopped for coffee. Running into Paul was something she could have happily avoided for the rest of her life.

During the drive back to the Kallis factory, she replayed their conversation in her head. Good for

Damon, for biting Paul's head off. For the first time, she appreciated his surly demeanor. No doubt, Paul had worded his question in a way to elicit anger. Ambush and attack had always been his M.O.

Bright sunlight beat into the car, increasing the pain in her head like someone was grinding a screwdriver into her temple. She grabbed her coffee and her bag, and hustled through the cold and into the warmth of the building. She needed some ibuprofen.

Her phone chimed with a text when she reached the reception area. Damon's name on the display sent equal parts excitement and annoyance through her.

Damon: In a meeting with my parents. Should be wrapped up by noon.

Great. What was she supposed to do for the next hour—hang around the break room until he'd finished? Maybe she should just drive home.

Annoyed beyond measure, she was tempted to send him the question but held off on the sarcasm.

Emily: Fine. I'm back from the meeting with the caterer. I guess I'll wait in the break room. As usual.

She stuffed her phone in her purse. The break room wasn't a bad idea. She needed to reheat her latte and find something small, like crackers, to take with her pain meds.

The scent of fresh-brewed coffee wafted into the hall from the break room. She entered, and the overhead light magnified the pulsing in her head. A big part of her wanted to take a sick day and head home, but the thought of facing all that bright sunshine again was too much.

Aidan stood by the coffee maker. He turned, and she winced as the light from the window flashed against the coffee pot he held. "Hey. How's it going?"

"All right, I guess."

"Are you sure? You look like you're not feeling too good."

"I have a headache." After punching in some numbers into the microwave to heat her latte, she fed a dollar into the vending machine for a pack of crackers. The microwave's beeping didn't help the pain throbbing in her skull. She ate a cracker, then downed two pills.

Aidan's brow creased in concern. "Do you want to go home? You can take a half day. I know the orientation paperwork said new hires don't get personal time for the first thirty days, but you can always make up a couple of hours. We don't expect you to be here if you're sick or not feeling well."

"No. That's okay. Even with sunglasses on, the sunlight is too much to deal with right now. I'd rather take some meds and give them a chance to work first."

"All right. But if you change your mind, just send me a message before you leave. I know it's pretty bright in here, but at least Damon's office has those automatic shades. He won't care if you need to lower them."

She barely held back a snort of derision. Maybe Damon wouldn't mind if it were for his friends. But for her? She wouldn't hold her breath. Since Aidan was staring at her expectantly, she nodded. "I'll ask him when he's back from his meeting."

"You don't need his permission to lower the blinds." He glanced at the clock on the wall. "Actually, I can come with you now in case you need help with them. The button for the blinds on the one side of the office occasionally sticks, and I'm tall enough to manually pull it down."

"I can't go now. His office is locked."

His brows drew together. "You don't have a key yet?"

She shook her head.

Aidan's lips twisted into a frown. "I have a key. I can let you in."

"I know he doesn't like anyone being in his office if he's not there." She liked Aidan and didn't want him to get in trouble.

"Then he can yell at me. You work here. Your desk is in there. You need a key. Come on. That meeting should be finishing up soon anyway."

She appreciated the support. Aidan walked with her to the office and unlocked the door. He shook his head as they entered the space, but didn't say anything until he reached the blinds. One worked perfectly, rolling down without much of a sound. The other stuck, as Aidan had said, but he pulled it down in one smooth movement. Then he headed toward the door. "I'll text him, so he knows. And I'll remind him that you need a key. I hope you feel better soon."

"Thanks, Aidan. For everything."

He nodded and walked away.

She did need a key. And she needed to prove she could handle more than party planning. Rearranging his desk was out of the question. She'd never do that without asking and he kept things relatively neat anyway.

The line of boxes against the wall would be the best place to start. Damon had mentioned that he needed to go through them. She pulled one box away from the rest and dragged it over to her desk. Organizing it would be her first order of business.

The pain in her head teamed up with nausea and made muscling through impossible. Craving dark and quiet just until the pain pills kicked in, she locked the door, then turned off the lights, and laid her head on her desk.

Stress was responsible for the pain, and she needed to figure out how to deal with Damon. The best start would be to lose the headache and get her emotions under control before she ended up doing or saying something she regretted.

She had a feeling they'd resume their fight once he returned to the office and she needed to be prepared.

CHAPTER FIVE

Damon glanced at the sunlight streaming through the window of the conference room. Bright and cheerful, it was the opposite of how he'd felt for weeks. And after that morning's altercation with Emily, he felt even worse. He turned his attention back to his parents and sister. "Research and Development is making strides in improving the toy. The bigger model will allow more room for the battery. No more overheating. No more explosions."

Their mother nodded and made a note on the paper in front of her. "I'm glad. Even with the recall, the company will come through okay. I think consumers appreciated our honesty and how quickly we moved and how fast we're processing the refunds."

He wasn't quite as optimistic. "We'll see…"

"What about the holiday bonuses?" Kira picked up her coffee mug. "Are they off the table or will they be delayed? I'm happy to forgo mine if it helps."

Their dad shook his head. "Our employees work hard. They deserve the bonus. I know some of them depend on it to pay for family presents or festivities. Bonuses will still happen."

"Good." Damon stood and stretched. "I guess that wraps it up."

"Not so fast." Kira set down her mug. "We need to talk about Emily."

Their mom smiled and glanced from Kira to Damon. "She's such a nice woman. How's she working out?"

Damon shrugged. No way did he want to talk about her, or how she'd laid into him that morning. The things she'd said had ticked him off. Mostly because she'd been right.

All the times he'd waved off her help or sent her away, and all the times he'd kept quiet or withdrew into himself, his intention had been self-preservation. And now that he was looking at it from her point of view, he felt awful.

His attraction to her had grown the more time they spent together. Her personality was as beautiful as her looks. He wanted her so much. But the thought of getting involved—even as friends, of being vulnerable once again, *scared* him…

Kira stood and slapped her hands on the table. "Emily is miserable. Damon hasn't made her feel welcome. He's hardly given her a single thing to do besides double-check the charity gala and employee holiday party information, even though she's been begging for more. She also doesn't have a key to his office because he doesn't want anyone in there if he's not around, so she's stuck in the break room. A lot."

"Damon." His dad's gruff scold made him feel like a ten-year-old boy rather than a thirty-five-year-old vice president of a successful corporation.

Eyes sparking fire, his sister pointed at him. "She thinks you don't like her, and that you think she's not capable of the job. She's brilliant. I wouldn't have suggested her if I didn't think she could do it. But more than that, she's my best friend, and we take care of our friends, just like you've always taken care of Hunter and Aidan. You better fix this, Damon."

He sank into his seat. His stomach felt like a lead weight. "I wasn't aiming to make her miserable."

For a long moment, no one spoke. Then his dad rounded the table and patted him on the shoulder. "You'll fix it."

The words somehow came out as sounding like both a comfort and a command.

"You can't let what happened with Ursula keep messing with your head." Kira's words cut straight to his gut. He'd been an idiot with Ursula, and it had cost him nearly everything.

And now it was messing up any possibility of a relationship—professional or otherwise—with Emily. He needed to pull himself back together. "I know. I'll fix it."

His mom hugged him. "I know you will. I raised a good man. But for goodness sake, give the poor girl a key to your office."

Laughter huffed out, shaky and unsure as he returned the hug. His office was his fortress, his retreat. He'd held off on handing over a key because once he did, that security would vanish.

When Kira met his gaze, he offered her a smile. "Thanks for helping me pull my head out of my ass, kid."

After promising to follow up soon with another progress report, strode out of the room. Once Emily came back, he could apologize and try to make things right. His phone buzzed in his pocket, a reminder of the messages he'd ignored during the meeting. He pulled it free and found a text from Emily, letting him know that she'd returned from the caterer meeting and would be waiting in the break room, and another, delivered minutes after Emily's, from Aidan.

Aidan: I let Emily into your office. Dude, either give her a key, or I'll move her someplace where she won't need you to access her desk. Enough is enough.

Damn it. No one was happy with him. He tucked the phone away and walked faster. Greeting his team as he passed, he drummed up a smile. That fell away when his office doorknob wouldn't turn.

What the hell? She'd locked *him* out?

Swearing low, annoyance racing through him, he unlocked and then opened the door. A darkened room greeted him, the blinds drawn shut against the afternoon sun. His eyes adjusted to the shadows. Emily sat at her desk, head down, resting on her hands. Dark hair pooled around her so he couldn't see her face.

Again—what the hell?

He pulled the door closed, none too gently, then flipped the lights on.

An anguished cry filled the air, and Emily raised her head. Her hands lifted to her temples, and she winced. "Please don't yell at me. I need a few more minutes before I'll be able to fight with you."

He had zero intention of yelling. Her careful, deliberate movements and pained expression had captured his attention. "Want to tell me why you're sitting here in the dark?"

"Because the light was making my headache worse. As soon as the pain meds kick in, we can fight all you want." Her whispered words and the grimace on her face when she massaged her forehead tugged at something deep in his chest.

He flipped off the light and then sank to his knees by her side and kept his tone low. "Migraine?"

"Maybe. Or a stress headache."

Stress he'd no doubt caused. He thought about everything Kira had said. His guilt tripled. "Anything I can do for you?"

"Don't be angry at Aidan for letting me in. And I know you don't like anyone in your office when you're not here, but when I came back from meeting with the hotel, my head hurt so bad and—"

"Shh. It's fine." He clasped her hand and lifted his other hand to stroke the hair at her temple. "You relax. We can stay here like this for as long as you need."

Her eyes fluttered closed. "That feels nice."

"Then I'll keep doing it." He shifted his weight, perched on the edge of the desk, and his hip pressed into her hand. The he remembered the small heating pad he kept in his desk in case Hunter was having a bad day, pain-wise. After retrieving it, he plugged it into the outlet behind Emily's desk and then held the soft cloth-covered pad to her forehead. Their fingers brushed as she took hold of the pad. He kept stroking her hair, anything to keep her relaxed and, hopefully, to keep her mind off of the pain, all the while berating himself for being such an ass and causing her stress.

The box of files on her desk made him pause. "What were you doing with the files?"

"I thought I'd go through and organize them. You mentioned you'd been meaning to do it. I just wanted to help."

They held toy sketches and ideas he'd brainstormed. No one outside of a select few had seen them before. The plans for the new teddy bear prototype were in there too. Hopefully, she hadn't come across them. He needed to move the boxes to his apartment, or lock the files in his desk until he had time to scan and then shred them. But he wouldn't tell her that, especially not now. "How far did you get?"

"Not very. I'm not a slacker. I tried to work through this, but I couldn't."

"Don't worry about any of that." Stress always caught him in the back of his neck, at the base of his skull. And when she shifted one hand to massage her nape, he couldn't help asking, "Can I help? Two hands can cover twice the amount of muscles."

"Um, sure. If you want. I mean, we have known each other for years. It's not like I just met you for the first time two weeks ago. If you're worried about me thinking it's anything inappropriate, I don't. Not at all. I just want to feel better as fast as I can, and you can help make that happen."

He was nervous to touch her. Had wanted to touch her all along, ever since that first day. He hadn't touched a woman in any way since Ursula. He slipped his fingers along her delicate neck and stroked the slope where it met her shoulders, and then up the back of her neck. Gentle circles, careful touches, soothing the tight muscles. It was the least he could do.

He'd made this happen, and he needed to fix it.

Her hand, warm on his side, was one more connection, almost like she wanted to keep him close. He liked the weight of it against him. Hell, he liked her. And it was time to stop punishing her for someone else's sins.

Her eyes, that deep chocolate gaze, watched him. Slowly, her muscles relaxed and the tension in her features slipped away.

For a while—minutes, maybe an hour—he ignored the buzzing of his phone, and the workload mounting on his desk, caught in the quiet stillness of taking care of Emily.

When the angle of the sun slanted, she shifted, and her focus landed to where she touched his leg. Faint pink flushed in her cheeks, and she moved her hand away. "It's much better now. Thank you."

He forced his hands away from her smooth skin but stayed where he was. "We need to talk."

"All right." Her lips pressed together for a moment, and then she nodded and straightened in her chair.

He hated the thought that she'd feel the need to steel herself against him. "I need to apologize. I haven't made your job easy."

She gaped at him, and he couldn't blame her. After how he'd acted, an apology was the last thing she probably expected. "True."

He shoved his hand through his hair. "I've been sort of a dick, and that's not right. I promise to be better."

"Does this mean you'll give me more things to do?"

"I will."

"What about my own key?"

"That too." Knowing she had one would be hard to handle, but he nodded. His problem, not hers. "And I'm okay with you being in here alone when I'm not here."

She laid her hand over his. "I understand what it's like to have someone invading your personal space, and I promise I won't take advantage of that."

She understood, and he was grateful. "I'll show you more of what my previous assistant handled, and then add things on as we go."

Or, as his trust in her grew.

Her brows lifted. "That's a big change from how it's been for the past two weeks, or even from this morning."

He shrugged. "My family's not afraid to point out when I'm acting like a jerk. You aren't either."

Her eyes closed and she groaned. Her hand slipped away, leaving his cold. "Kira said something, didn't she?"

"She was right to do it. And so were you." He shifted until their hands touched once more. "I don't like being called out."

"I can't imagine anyone does."

"But it was needed in this case. I'm sorry. With the teddy bear catastrophe, I'm having trouble seeing past my own issues." He couldn't tell her about Ursula. Not yet. Probably not ever.

"Apology accepted." Her forgiving smile came easy, blooming across her face like sunlight breaking through clouds.

And those curved lips beaconed to his suppressed desires. He wanted to feel them under his. Wanted it more than breathing. That overwhelming need hadn't happened in forever. Not since he'd closed off that part of himself. Emily was breaking through his locks, pushing open doors he'd intended to remain closed.

Could he again? *Should* he?

Loneliness was an acute pain in his chest. He missed the closeness of being with someone.

Those luscious lips parted, and her eyes darkened.

His heartbeat quickened, galloping in his chest. Ramping up for something big. The adrenaline rush matched what he felt when speeding down the ice, flying toward the goal. But it was bigger than that. It was more. Anticipation and desire mixed with the unknown.

He brushed his fingers along the side of her face and then cradled it in his hand. Moving slow, he bent over her.

Closer.

Closer.

Her hand slid up his chest and pushed, stopping him cold. He braced his other arm on the back of her chair and waited. Had he misread, or seen something that wasn't there?

Her eyes were eloquent—so much emotion swirled in her chocolate gaze. "We don't want to make a mistake."

"Mistake?"

"Jumping into something we might regret later."

"I don't think I'd ever regret kissing you." But he eased back to give her breathing room. Maybe he had rushed, jumped too fast. "You keep resting here until you're feeling better. Don't worry about anything else. I'll be at my desk, but I'll be quiet. And we'll leave the lights off until you can stand them."

Her fingers curled into his shirt. "Wait. Please."

He complied, resting a hip on the desk.

"This is just... sudden... I mean, this morning, I was ready to throttle you for being so difficult, and now here we are, you're apologizing and promising, and then we're practically kissing in your office. It's a huge jump." She stood up, using his shirt as leverage, and the position brought her much closer to him.

Closer than they'd been when he'd moved in for the kiss.

"So what are you saying?"

"I'm saying that getting involved with someone you work with but don't know that well may not be a smart idea."

He had a pretty good idea that she was referring to her experience with the co-worker at the TV station. "I get it. And I agree."

Her fingers flexed a little on his shirt, reminding him that she'd yet to let go. "I'm not saying I don't want to kiss you. I do. But I think we should see how we work together, now that we'll actually be working together if you're serious about including me. We should get to know each other a little better now that things will be more open before we try anything else."

He could do that. He appreciated her caution, liked that she wanted to get to know him better, and definitely understood where she was coming from. If he'd been more cautious about his ex, then maybe he could've prevented much of the heartaches and headaches. "You've got yourself a deal."

Emily's smile returned. "I'm feeling better if you want to get started."

He didn't want to move from her desk or the intimacy of their position or their deep conversation, but he did have a mountain of work calling his name. "How about we start with you giving me the run down on the party planning."

For the next hour, they worked, huddled close

together, laptops open at his desk. He kept the overhead light off and opened the blinds enough for them to easily see their keyboards. No way would he chance anything that might bring back her headache. He gave her access to his calendar and schedule and taught her how to navigate parts of the system.

Then he glanced at the clock. "We should break for lunch. How's your head?"

"Headache's gone." She set aside the pad and pen she'd used for taking notes. For the first time, he realized the pen had candy cane stripes and dancing snowmen, and she'd affixed a snowflake sticker to her laptop.

"Getting into the Christmas spirit already?"

"I love Christmas. I put my tree up and decorated my house the day after Thanksgiving."

He didn't decorate his place. Didn't see the point when it was just for him. "Kira, Hunter, Aidan, and I are decorating the lobby after hours one night later this week. You're welcome to help if you want to stick around."

"Sure. Sounds like fun." She glanced around his office, and he thought he knew what was coming next. "What about in here?"

Yep, he'd guessed that one correctly.

He followed her gaze. The only holiday things he'd ever displayed were cards he received. But her hopeful expression melted any resistance he had. "Never have, but you're welcome to put some things on your desk or do whatever you want."

Her smile was his reward. He could get addicted to

seeing that happiness on her face, and the knowledge that he'd put it there.

A brief knock sounded against his door, then it opened without waiting for an invite. Kira, Hunter, and Aidan stood in the doorway, faces expectant. He smiled and leaned closer to Emily, hoping to convey that he'd made an effort to fix things. "We've been working pretty hard in here. You guys ready for lunch?"

His sister pushed in first, eyes darting from him to Emily, and back again before her tense expression eased. "Mexican, Italian, or Thai food?"

He brushed his fingertips over the back of Emily's hand—a quick caress over soft skin that made him want more. "New girl gets to choose."

Emily tapped her finger to her chin, as if considering, but only twice before blurting her answer. "Italian."

"Big surprise," Kira teased. She smiled, and when they exited the room, she grabbed Damon's arm and mouthed *thank you*.

He nodded and then shifted until he was walking beside Emily.

For the first time in forever, he felt like himself.

His past no longer would control his future.

CHAPTER SIX

Slats of early morning sunshine cut through the tree branches and striped the floor of the break room. The clean white cabinet glowed cheerily. Even the coffee maker shined brighter, at least to Emily. She set down the box of decorations she'd brought in from home and rooted through the cabinet until she'd found her snowman mug. She filled it, then sat, sipping the brew while she waited for Damon.

He'd promised to hunt down a spare key to his temporary office. The one his former assistant had used was for the office currently being renovated.

Since their conversation two days earlier, and his promise about the key, and his including her in more tasks, she didn't mind waiting for him anymore. Kira had mentioned that Damon had trust issues, but in spite of them, he seemed to be trying. Considering she'd developed trust issues of her own, she'd have to cut him some slack.

He walked in, dressed in a black shirt rolled to the elbows and dark gray pants. They would be a coordinated pair today, with her in a light gray wool dress and black tights and boots.

"Morning." He smiled and headed for the pot. "Sorry I'm late. I stopped by the hardware store on my way in. I had a key made for you."

"You did?" She stood, brushing the wrinkles from her dress.

"Here." He held out a red and white striped key.

Her nerve endings sizzled when their fingers touched. "It's cute. Reminds me of a candy cane."

"You mentioned you liked Christmas. I thought of you when I saw this one."

Her heart melted at the thoughtfulness of his gesture. "Thank you."

"What's in the box?" He added creamer to his coffee, then joined her at the table.

"Just a few decorations."

"I'll carry that. You take the coffees."

Once inside his office, she set the coffees on their desks. "I have something for you, too."

"Yeah?"

She reached into the box and pulled out a twelve-inch mini-Christmas tree, complete with lights. "Here."

His brows rose, and the corner of his lip quirked in a smile. "Thanks."

"It's battery operated, and there's a switch for blinking or steady lights." She handed it over and smiled when he turned the lights on and placed the tree on the end of his desk.

"What about for you?"

"I have one too." She set a matching tree on her desk. Then hung a large red bow decorated with jingle bells from the doorknob. They would ring like a Santa Claus arrival every time someone opened or closed the door. "There, all done. That didn't take long."

Twinkling, colorful lights on two green pine trees made the small drab room much cheerier. She'd held off on bringing in anything else because the room really was short on space.

Damon leaned on the edge of his desk. "It looks good in here."

"I think so too." She picked up her coffee, pleased that he'd been open about the decorations. "What's on the schedule for today, besides decorating the main lobby later?"

"I have some reports I need to run, and I'll need you to do some research for me. We'll get to them soon." He glanced behind her and his brows drew together. "But first, where are the boxes that were lined up along the wall?"

Her gaze flicked to the empty space. "I scanned and then shredded them yesterday afternoon."

"What?" He crossed the space between their desks faster than she'd ever seen him move.

Frowning, she set the coffee aside. "You mentioned a week ago that you needed to find some time to go through the boxes and organize, scan, and then shred everything, so I did it while you were at your meeting with the lawyer." He hadn't returned to the office because the meeting had ran so late. Aidan had shown up at five-thirty and locked the office door when she left. She crossed her arms over her chest. Why was he so angry? "I organized the papers into separate folders. One for designs, one for plans, and one for miscellaneous."

"Where did you save the information?"

She pulled the stick drive out of her desk drawer and tossed it to him. "There you go. And I also backed it up to your folder on the cloud server."

He palmed the drive and tucked it into his pocket, rounding her desk until only her chair separated them. "Who helped you carry the boxes to the shredder room? Did you let someone else shred them?"

Gripping the back of her chair, she resisted the urge to back up. "I did it myself."

"Don't lie to me."

His anger touched off her own. "You think I can't carry a box?"

"Don't put words in my mouth. If someone helped you carry, I need to know. Same goes if you let someone else shred them."

"I swear, I did it all. Why? What's the big deal?"

"The big deal is that the papers contain confidential information. I'm sure you saw the new plans for the teddy bear in there."

"I did."

He leaned forward and laid his hands over hers, and

she could feel the strength in his grip. "There's a reason why they were in here, under lock and key. We can't have that kind of information floating around."

"I scanned everything myself. And I took the boxes to the shredder room one at a time and shredded them myself. It took me about four hours."

"But the office was unlocked each time you left." A muscle in his jaw jumped. "You signed a nondisclosure form when you were hired. You can't talk about anything that's under development with anyone outside the company. Those papers you saw contain past and future plans, and some other sensitive information that only certain people in the company are privy to seeing. You can't talk about what's in there with anyone besides me, my parents, Kira, Aidan, Hunter, and a couple of people on the creative and design teams."

She raised a brow. "Aidan and Hunter. So, a guy from HR and a guy from IT are included in on possible design sketches and prototype plans?" She knew they were really close to Damon and Kira, but hadn't realized that they were involved in nearly every aspect of the business.

His fingers tightened and his eyes burned. "They're like my brothers. I trust them with everything. Not that I need to explain my reason for including them."

"Message received." Her words snapped out, and she tugged to free her hands from his grip. He guarded his privacy with the ferocity of a lion defending its territory, and not being included in his circle of trust cut deeper than she'd expected.

After a long moment, he sighed. "I wish you'd told me before you did it."

"You were in your meeting, I didn't want to disturb you, and I ran out of things to do. I wasn't going to sit here goofing off for four hours. I figured you would be happy that I took something off your plate. But once again, I'm wrong." And here, she'd thought they'd been making real progress.

Light came into his eyes, clearing the anger from his dark gaze. "I'm sorry. I was way out of line. I tend to blow up first and then react calmly later. I'm trying to work on that, but obviously failed here. You did something to help me, and I appreciate it."

She blinked, not expecting his apology. "Really?"

He rubbed his hands over his face. "This recall and trying to get the replacement toy ready has been eating at me. So much is at stake. If the information gets leaked and someone beats us to the punch, the likelihood that we'd have to do a layoff increases by a lot. This company and its people mean everything to me. I can't let anything happen to it or them."

He looked exhausted. The morning sunlight streamed over the lines of stress in his face. She could understand where he was coming from. He was a hothead, a tough guy, but had a soft heart. She touched his cheeks and then smoothed her fingers over those lines. "I promise I won't talk about anything I see here to anyone besides you, and Kira, and the guys."

His eyes closed for a moment, and then he pinned her with his serious brown stare and captured her wrists in his hands. "I don't seem to be able to make a good impression on you."

"It's all right. I keep reminding myself that I've really known you for years and that up until recently, you were pretty friendly and a little flirty with me. All of that time outweighs the few instances where you've been… challenging…"

"I guess *challenging* is better than *asshole*." His thumb stroked over her pulse. Could he feel it beating faster? He slowly lowered her hands, but kept them bound in his. "I'm sorry I hit the roof."

"You seem to only hit the roof when something matters, and I get that. I'm sorry too. I should have run it by you first. From now on, I promise to let you know before I grab anything new to do."

"And I promise, no more breakdowns in communication from my side either. Still, I feel bad. This is the second time this week I'm apologizing to you. You deserve better than that, and I promise, I'll be better."

She wanted to lighten the mood. He'd apologized. She'd apologized. Now, they needed to move forward. "Can I listen to Christmas music in here? I've noticed you never have music playing."

"If you want music, you can have music. You can have anything you want." He let go of her wrists and then brought one hand to her face and framed it. "We're really okay? You're not going to quit on me, or something, are you?"

Did he really care about her, or was he worried

about his family's reaction if she quit? "We're fine. I promise."

"Good." His mouth curved in a tentative smile. "Because I really like having you here."

Did he mean that? She wanted to believe it. Her heart warmed at the hope in his eyes. "I like it too."

Eight hours later, she stood on a small ladder in the main lobby, helping Kira hang a long strand of garland around the front doors.

On the other side, out in the cold, Damon and Hunter draped a corresponding strand, and then hung two large wreaths. No matter what she did, she was still aware of his nearness, as though they weren't separated by a thick pane of glass.

Behind her, Aidan and his fiancée Skye decorated a tall, artificial tree with white lights and red and green ornaments.

Emily stepped off the ladder, careful of her heeled boots. "That looks good."

Kira nodded. "And we have a bowl of cinnamon-scented pine cones to set on the reception desk. Wait until tomorrow—it's going to smell like Christmas in here."

Skye joined them, rubbing her hands over her arms. "It's chilly over here. Nice work. The door looks great."

Emily moved the ladder out of the way. She'd met Skye a handful of times over the last few months. The delicate blonde bore burn scars on the left side of her body but possessed the quiet strength of a survivor. A victim of a horrible fire, she'd fled to Holiday, fell in love with Aidan, and he always said she saved him as much as he saved her.

The chill increased when Damon opened the door, letting in himself, Hunter, and a gust of cold wind. Hunter shuffled by, rubbing his hand on the outside of his thigh. Kira had mentioned that he still suffered nerve pain from bullet wounds he'd sustained while in the Army. Cold weather aggravated his injuries. Groaning, he shook his head. "Running tomorrow morning is going to suck."

Damon clapped him on the shoulder. "You can skip it if you need to."

"Is everyone else going to be there?" He raised his brows at the group. Aidan, Skye, Kira, and Damon all nodded. "Well then, I'll be there too."

Murmuring what sounded like *stubborn man*, Kira turned to Emily. "You should come too."

Kira had invited her a few times over the years, but her schedule hadn't allowed it, and she didn't think she'd enjoy running at the crack of dawn. But, she'd just gotten in good graces with Damon, and the rest of the group seemed to support her, so even if the idea of waking up early and punishing her body in the cold wasn't appealing, she needed to do it. "I've never really run before, but I walk a sub-fifteen-minute mile on a regular basis, so jogging shouldn't be too hard."

"We're not joggers." Damon managed to look

offended but then followed his indignation with a wink and a smile.

"Oh, that's right. I'd heard that some runners hate being labeled as joggers."

Skye's gentle laughter trickled over. "I'm fine with whatever label you use, but the rest of this crew is pretty hardcore."

"I might be slow enough to fall into jogger category." Hunter rubbed his leg again, wearing a rueful smile.

Kira slipped her arm around his waist. "You do just fine."

The love on her face sent twin shards of jealousy and longing through Emily. She busied herself with tidying up stray strands of garland. Was she happy for Kira? Of course. But more and more, she felt like she'd never find something as deep as Kira and Hunter shared.

Damon joined her, resting his hand on her shoulder. She felt his warmth through the material of her dress. "So, tomorrow. We'll meet at the trail just off the highway entrance to town. We start at six-thirty. If you're running late, call me."

It would still be dark at that hour, not to mention that she usually slept until seven-thirty. "I'll be there."

Maybe not fully awake. But that hadn't been a requirement.

The next morning, Emily pulled into the trail's parking lot, exactly on time, and still the last to arrive. Stifling a yawn, she climbed out of her car. Staying up late the night before, wrapping gifts for her sisters and watching a Christmas movie, had seemed like a good idea at the time, but five hours sleep wasn't enough.

Kira grinned and waved. "You made it."

"It's so early, it doesn't feel real." She grabbed her water bottle and shivered in the crisp air.

"You get used to it."

Damon smiled at her, and her body warmed in spite of the cold. "You're new to running. It's best if you have a gait analysis, but I can try to help for now." He walked closer and then touched her shoulders. "You want to run like your body is being pulled up by a string. Shoulders back, good posture." Then his hand snaked down her spine, and she felt the touch through the two layers she wore. "Keep your hands below your heart, so it's not working too hard to pump." He brought her one hand up and then stopped it at low-chest level. "And, try landing on your mid-foot rather than on your heels or toes, so there's less stress on your knees." He ended with touching her knee.

Emily swallowed at the rush of heat from Damon's hands-on tutorial.

Not the time, nor the place.

Kira met her gaze, and her friend's raised brows suggested Emily would be fielding questions soon.

Damon tapped his water bottle against hers. "We're doing the five-mile loop, but if it's too much, there's a turn off for the three-mile loop at the first mile-marker. Just take it easy. Don't push too fast right out of the gate. And the wind will dehydrate you, so remember to drink your water."

"Damon, enough. She gets it." Kira pushed in, forcing Damon to back away. "You're going to over-whelm her, and she'll never come again."

He leveled a glance at his sister. "If she's not prop-erly informed, she could get hurt or tired or dehydrated, and not want to come again either."

"Guys, it's fine." Emily smiled at them both, then touched Damon's arm. "Thanks for the tips."

He grinned and his eyes crinkled at the corners. "No problem."

Then, he walked toward Aidan and Skye. "Let's go."

Emily followed behind with Kira and Hunter. The group took off together, but within seconds, the front three had pulled ahead.

Two minutes in, Emily's lungs were screaming for a break. How the hell did anyone think this was fun? She was hot, uncomfortable, and miserable. Running was so very different from walking, even the speed walking she did.

Puffing, she slowed her pace.

Kira glanced at her and followed suit. "I'm sorry about my brother. Damon likes to take charge."

"No kidding. But it was sweet." She gulped air. Seri-ously—how was Kira not even breathing hard?

Hunter slowed on Kira's other side. "He's always been that way. He likes making sure that everyone is taken care of. He gave Aidan and me a job when we got out of the Army, and has always included us like we're family. Don't be offended by his taking control, it comes from a good place."

"I can see that now." They'd really been working well together for the past several days, even with his idiosyncrasies, and despite that minor blow-up in his office the day before. "You guys don't have to slow down for me. I'll be okay. Maybe I'll walk to the two-and-a-half marker and then turn around, and meet you all back at the start. You'll probably have completed the loop by then. I'm a faster walker than I am a jogger so we might finish at the same time."

"I'm not fast. And Kira's stuck with me for years. We're fine with going slow." Hunter winced and rubbed at his thigh. "We usually pair off like this. The three up ahead will eventually turn back this way to meet up with us. No one leaves anyone behind."

They continued on, alternating walking and jogging for thirty-second intervals, short enough to be manage-able, even bearable. One mile down, then two, then three. Emily ducked her head against a gust of wind. Winter was in the air.

"So…" Kira nudged her arm. "What's up with you and my brother? I'm happy that he's not a jerk anymore, but you're both kind of touching each other a lot now."

Fresh heat that had nothing to do with exertion flushed into her cheeks. She knew Kira shared every-thing with Hunter, but she hadn't expected to have this conversation in front of him. Emily took a drink from her water bottle, but the cold water didn't help cool her down. "I don't know. We're attracted to each other, but we're being cautious and agreed to get to know each other better before we add in anything else."

"Agreed, as in you had a discussion about it?"

"Well, yeah."

"Holy shit." Hunter busted out a hoot. "Sorry. It's been a long while for him, that's all. He was hurt pretty bad. I'm happy he's starting to move on from that."

"From conversations with Kira, I only know the gist of what happened with his ex, but I think it's his place to tell me more if he wants. We know we've both had bad experiences, though, so if anything happens, I think we'd be careful to make sure we don't hurt each other."

Soon enough, three figures loped toward them—Damon in his bright red shirt and black pants, Aidan entirely in black, and Skye in teal and gray.

Damon grinned at her. "Having fun?"

"Sure."

Kira nudged her arm again. "Thirty seconds is up. Back to walking."

"Walking?" Damon moved to Emily's other side. Worry creased his features. "Did you get a cramp? Pull a muscle? Are you okay?"

"I'm just not used to running." She felt like the slowest kid in gym class all over again.

The entire group reduced their speed to walking. The trail was too narrow to walk six-across, so Aidan and Skye walked ahead of them.

Damon slid his arm around her shoulders. "None of us were banging out miles when we first started."

Skye turned around. "I wouldn't mind walking with

you on some days, Emily. It's good to change things up."

"Me too." Kira nodded.

"Thanks." Although she'd been Kira's friend for years, her inclusion in this group was pretty new. Even so, she felt completely comfortable with all of them.

Damon jostled her gently by the shoulders, insisting on her attention. She glanced over at him, his flushed face serious. "And if you want to get your body used to running, I can help you. We can put together a plan later when we get into the office."

The image of them sitting together huddled close over a single laptop—hands brushing at the keyboard, thighs touching below the desk—convinced her of the right answer. Instead, she said, "Yes. That would be great."

CHAPTER SEVEN

Damon sat at his desk, thoroughly distracted by Emily. She'd looked so cute on the trail that morning, hair pulled into a high ponytail, in her black leggings and purple sweatshirt. He liked the office version just as much. Emily bent over her laptop, typing intently. Her crisp, white button-down shirt tucked into a red skirt, hinted at her curves just enough to drive him crazy picturing the rest of her.

Over cups of coffee and his laptop, he'd helped her put a running plan together, imagining them on dates at the running trail. She'd jotted down notes as he'd talked about everything from nutrition to interval training to cool-down stretches. Maybe he'd talked too much, but with her so close to him, and her scent teasing his nose, and her shoulder warm under his fingers, he kept speaking until he'd exhausted the topic and was running late to a board meeting.

The buzzing of his phone pulled him out of his

musing. He looked at the text from Caleb, his lead engineer. *Hey, boss. We just completed the production-ready prototype, if you want to check it out.*

Awesome! This could be the best morning he'd had in ages. Damon pushed away from his desk. "The new prototype's ready. Want to come with me to check it out?"

Emily's smile spread easily and lit up her face. Yeah, he could get addicted to those smiles. One from her held enough power to light up his entire day. "What about the research you wanted? I'm not finished yet."

"Let it wait." He got to his feet and waved for her to get up. "You haven't seen the design room yet. It's the coolest place in the whole building."

"Sure." Emily stood and stretched. "Ever since I saw the sketches in the folder, I've been curious about the new bear."

When they reached Research & Development, he paused outside the door. "Remember, that nondisclosure form applies to anything you see behind these doors."

"I understand."

"Then let's have some fun." He held the door for her and then followed her into the large, bright room. At table after table, people worked on models, sketched designs on paper, or used computers.

"Our design team includes a mix of artists, sculptors, engineers, and craftsmen, with backgrounds in toys and video games." Damon kept his hand on her back as he guided her through the room and made the introductions. As he'd expected, everyone greeted her warmly and offered her a chance to play with their new creations. He was so proud of his team, and not just of all they'd accomplished.

Emily flipped a switch on a hand-held controller and sent a remote control sports car into a 360 skid then rolled it back to the designer. She handed over the controller and thanked him, grinning like a kid at Christmas. "So. Where's the bear?"

"I'll show you." He led her to the back of the room, toward Caleb, his lead engineer. "Caleb, meet Emily, my new assistant."

They shook hands, then Damon said, "His daughter Gwen is a big fan of the stuffed animals we make."

"Her favorite is the orange-striped kitten." Caleb pointed to a photo of a dark-haired little girl in a hospital bed, hugging the stuffed animal. Seeing the concern on Emily's face, he elaborated. "She has leukemia. She's at Children's Hospital right now."

"I'm so sorry." Her face creased in sympathy. "I'll think good thoughts for her."

Damon patted him on the shoulder. He hated that the sweet little girl was sick, but Gwen was receiving some of the best care in the country. "Did she like the animal puzzles we sent over last week?"

Caleb smiled and nodded, and the worry in his eyes receded. "Anything with animals, she loves. That's why I can't wait for the prototype to be ready. She'll be over the moon for a bear that can move and talk to her."

"Soon, man. We'll get there."

"Maybe in time for Valentine's Day." Caleb's voice

was soft and strained, and his fingers plucked at the edge of his table, as though itching to get back to work.

While Damon appreciated the enthusiasm, he didn't need any careless mistakes. "If it's ready by then, that would be great. But I'm not rushing any step of this process."

"No, no. Of course not." Caleb's face reddened. "I didn't mean that we'd ignore any quality control procedures."

"Is this the new prototype?" Emily's voice pulled him back. She pointed to the plush brown bear lying on the table.

"It is." Caleb handed it over. "This is the production-ready sample. It has the final engineering completed, and from this, we'll make any finishing tweaks."

"And then you can sell them?"

"Not yet." Damon picked up the test phone and typed out a command, followed by *Hello, Emily.*

The bear's eyes opened. It waved its paw, and its mouth moved. "Hello, Emily."

She laughed and raised her smiling face to his. "That's great. I love it. Isn't that Skye's voice?"

"You have a good ear. It is. We put our resident voice over artist to work. We'll also be offering a male voice. And since Skye has the recording equipment at home, we convinced Aidan to give it a try. Of course, we also have recording equipment here, I have to show you that area too." He grinned. "The next step after this will be making the test toys, which are the first samples using the final materials we've selected. After that, we'll make the production sample, which is the final sample of the toy. Our group of toy testers will then come in and play with and review it. Then, we'll approve the final samples before we start production on the toys that will be sold to the public. We're probably still several months away from having a market-ready product."

Emily handed the bear to Caleb. "This is great. Thanks for letting me see it."

"Nice work, Caleb." Damon grinned at his engineer. "We'll make sure Gwen has an extra present when we visit the hospital on Friday. And if she's well enough when we get to the toy testers stage, we can bring it to her and let her take part."

"That would be great, boss."

Satisfied, Damon turned to Emily. "We'll be filling the gift bags for the kids tomorrow. Can you make sure we put aside an extra toy for Gwen?"

"Sure." She smiled at Caleb. "I can't wait to meet her."

"She's a good kid. Still managing to keep a smile on her face. I don't know how she does it."

An alert chimed and Emily pulled her phone from her pocket. Damon saw his calendar fill her screen. "I'm sorry. Damon, we'd better go. You have that lunch meeting soon."

He shook Caleb's hand. "We'll let you get back to work."

When they exited the room, Emily touched his arm. "It's so sweet that you care so much about his kid."

"He's worked here for over ten years. He's definitely part of the family. We'd do anything we could for that guy. It's a shame Gwen's sick, but she'll benefit from the check we'll be donating to the hospital. Actually, I'll let you in on a secret. Caleb doesn't know it yet, but the company is going to cover all of the costs of Gwen's treatment that aren't covered by insurance. I'm going to tell him at the employee Christmas party." Christmas Eve was the perfect time to give the present to one of his hardest-working employees.

"With the deductibles, copays, and co-insurance, I'm sure her costs are overwhelming. What a nice present."

"We take care of our people." He allowed himself to brush against her side as they entered the elevator. Opening up to Emily had become easy once he allowed his wall to come down. He wanted more. From her and from himself. But he'd have to wait until she was ready. He hoped it was soon. He'd wasted so much of his life waiting as it was.

The next day passed in a blur. Damon spent most of the day in meetings, and the refund and exchange program for teddy bear toy customers had hit a processing snag leading to enough hits on the company's website to crash the servers. Then, he'd had a phone call and an email from smarmy Paul Redmond of Channel 10, asking for an update on the second edition of the toy. No way was he returning that call. He forwarded it to the PR department.

Needing a smile, he stopped by to check in on Emily. She and several other employees were filling up the gift bags for the kids at Children's Hospital with toys. He spent a little while pitching in before his next meeting, with Emily working by his side, laughing, smiling, and lighting up the room with her presence. She'd proven herself to be far more than an adequate assistant, and he kept picturing scenarios that ended with them twined together like lights on a Christmas tree.

Thoughts of her kept his stress at bay for the rest of the day. By the time he arrived at Kira and Hunter's house to help decorate their tree later that evening, he was ready to unwind. Emily's car was already in the driveway, along with Aidan's SUV, which meant he was the last to arrive.

Kira threw the door open and holiday music spilled out into the night. "Come in."

"I brought beer and wine."

"And I thank you. After what happened with the website today, we all need a drink. Thank goodness that's fixed now." She stepped back and waved him inside. "Everyone's in the living room."

He followed the sound of voices. Hunter and Aidan stood by the TV, gazes fixated on a hockey game. Skye and Emily sat on the couch, looking through a box of ornaments. He set his bag on the coffee table. The urge to touch Emily welled huge within him.

She smiled at him. "I found one you made when you were a kid."

"Really?" He crouched by her side. The red and green painted ceramic wreath was tacky and ugly. "I guess artistic talent escaped me."

"It's cute."

"You really must like me, to say that." He was teasing, but her cheeks turned pink and her smile shy.

Kira set a tray of Christmas cookies on the coffee table. "Okay, people. This tree isn't going to decorate itself."

For the next half hour, he helped string lights and hang ornament after ornament on the tree. And watched his little sister and one of his best friends beam at their first Christmas tree together. So much had changed within their group over the last year, with Hunter engaged to Kira and Aidan engaged to Skye. He had to admit, at times, he felt a little like a fifth wheel.

Having Emily there helped, but it would help more if they actually were together. She chatted happily with him and was free with her touches to his hand and his back. But he hadn't yet earned the freedom to wrap his arm around her. And he wanted to hold her as much as he wanted to kiss her.

Hunter ordered pizzas, and as the group trooped into the kitchen to eat, Damon spied mistletoe hanging in a few doorways. He and Emily lagged behind everyone else. He pulled her aside, and under the doorway to the laundry room.

More than a little nervous she might reject him, he

pushed down all negative thoughts and took the biggest risk he'd had in months. His mouth as dry as the poly-fil they used to fill the Kallis Toys stuffed animals, he pointed to the little sprig of green above their heads. "Think we know each other well enough yet?"

Eyes on the mistletoe, she bit her lip but then she nodded. "I do."

His tight muscles eased. He'd gotten his chance, and he wouldn't waste it with a mere peck on the cheek. Damon traced his finger along her cheek, taking his time, learning the shape of her face. He wrapped his other hand around her shoulder, and the soft material of her sweater tickled his palm.

She leaned into him and rested her tapered fingers on his hip. Her brown eyes looked into his and then lowered to his mouth. He bent closer and her lips parted in response. Tucking her hair behind her ear, he lowered his head, his heart pounding like a drum.

Her eyes fluttered closed. He paused a breath away, so close he could almost feel her lips on his. Energy flowed through him, powering his muscles like his body knew he was on the verge of something big. He hadn't felt this way with any other woman. Maybe that was because there wasn't anyone exactly like Emily.

His lips closed over hers, and it was as though his heart had woken up for the first time. Everything felt *more*—his senses were alive with her scent, her taste, her body against his. Need and want moved through him as swift as a snow squall.

The cloying sweetness of cookies and wine lingered

on her tongue, but underneath he could still taste the tones of woman. And he wanted more. Sliding his hands through her thick hair, he cupped the back of her head.

Warm, soft, and perfect, she opened for him, slanting her head to accommodate him as he sought for a deeper taste. The brush of her tongue against his made his blood sing. His hands tightened, tugging her closer. Her hands traveled up his back and dug into his shirt, and he could feel her nails through the material. That dull pain ramped up his need.

His sister's voice broke in, calling out from the kitchen, asking if they were coming. The pizza must have arrived, yet he'd never heard the doorbell.

Damon raised his head, surprised that he felt a little off-balance. Emily held his gaze, her breathing unsteady. He traced his finger along her face once more, savoring the moment. "I guess that will have to hold me for now."

Emily slowly loosened her grip and smoothed his shirt. "I, ah, I'm glad we waited to do that."

She was right, waiting had made it mean more. But now, he wanted it again. And again.

He forced himself to lower his hand and take a step back. "We'd better head in before she comes out here."

"Right." She smoothed her sweater and then led the way into the kitchen.

He met his friends' curious glances with a smile, then made sure Emily had a drink and some pizza before getting his own beer and slices of the pepperoni pie. Still wearing that smile, he slid into the chair next to Hunter.

A year ago he wouldn't have seen himself with anyone ever again, but being with Emily felt so right. When she smiled at him from across the table, he could only hope that she felt the same.

Letting her in was scary and exhilarating and he needed to make sure he didn't do anything to screw it up.

CHAPTER EIGHT

Thick, gray clouds blanketed the sky and the threat of a weekend snowstorm charged the air. Stifling a yawn, Emily pulled into the trail's parking lot. When she stepped out of her car, the cold air stung her face, slapping her fully awake. She'd spent most of the night thinking about Damon and the kiss they'd shared. With all of the people around them when they'd said goodnight at Kira's house, they hadn't had any privacy to talk about it.

Damon strode up to her. "Morning."

"Hi." She tucked her keys away and shifted her weight from one foot to the other. Were they dating? Were they only kissing?

Longing for his touch, she glanced at the other two couples. The closeness they shared was something she yearned to have. The trail wasn't the place to have that conversation, not with an audience.

He bent his head and cupped her shoulders in his

hands, and her breath caught. Warm lips settled over hers, coaxing hers to part as they rubbed and teased.

Her pulse scrambled and then pounded. Her hands clutched his jacket and she pulled him closer. She deepened the kiss, chasing his flavor, until a low whistle pierced the air, reminding her that they weren't alone.

He lifted his head. "Ready to run again?"

"With lots of walking intervals? Yep."

Kira grinned at them. "Damon, it's too cold. I think we should do the short trail today."

Damon's gaze cut to Hunter. The blond man was walking with stiff movements, his hand on his thigh. "Agreed. That's better for Emily's training anyway."

Then he leaned down until his lips hovered by Emily's ear. "I'll slow my pace today, but if we get separated for too long, and you need to stop or if he's having too much trouble, text me."

"I will." She checked that her phone was secured in her zippered jacket pocket.

The group started out together, same as last time. But this time, Aidan, Damon, and Skye, kept turning back and meeting up with her, Kira, and Hunter. Aidan and Damon joked with Hunter, and she could see the concern, sympathy, and love in their words and actions. Damon might bark out orders or insist on taking charge, but everything he did seemed to stem from a desire to make sure everyone else was taken care of.

She fell for him a little bit further.

He kept checking on her too. And at the end of their run, he helped her stretch, guiding her through the movements. Attentive and caring, he made sure she knew the proper technique. She appreciated the undivided attention. Would be like this if they were truly together?

Getting involved with her boss was still a concern, but he'd been just Damon to her for far longer than the weeks he'd also had the title of boss, and she couldn't deny their chemistry or the way he made her feel.

He wasn't Paul.

He wouldn't hurt her the way her ex had.

A few hours later, Emily shivered in her coat as she helped load up Damon's SUV with gift bags for the Children's Hospital. Her body ached from the earlier run, but in a good way, and her spirits were high, from endorphins, or Damon, or a combination of both.

Behind her, a car door slammed. Damon's parents, Stan and Nadia would also be part of the gift-bearing caravan, along with Kira, Hunter, Aidan, and Skye. They were dividing up the floors at the hospital, and Gwen's floor had been promised to her and Damon. She tucked the extra toy into her purse, next to the Santa hat that Stan had handed out for everyone to wear.

"Ready?" Damon opened the passenger side door for her.

She climbed inside, sighing in approval of the heated seats. "I wish my car had these."

Rather than follow the other cars onto the highway,

Damon turned the car down a side street. "I need to grab a coffee. I didn't have any this morning. Jolt is close by. We should arrive at the hospital only a few minutes after the others."

"Sure. It's so cold, I wouldn't mind a second cup."

"One of the guys who I play hockey with owns the coffee shop. I try to stop in at least once a week to support him." He'd mentioned the hockey team a few times before. Hunter and Aidan and he all played on the same team in a men's rec league. Kira usually went to the games. Would Damon ever ask her to come?

The parking lot wasn't crowded, and Damon found a spot right in front. The shop was cute and smelled so good, of coffee and baked goods. Damon introduced her to Ben, the owner. He ordered a large regular coffee, then asked what she wanted. Torn between all the choices, she settled on a peppermint bark flavored coffee, drawn to the mint and chocolate.

Thick snowflakes were falling slowly when they exited the shop. Emily ducked her head to keep them off of her face as they walked to the car. "We were in there less than five minutes. The snow wasn't supposed to start this early, was it?"

"No." Frown creasing his features, Damon pulled the SUV back onto the street. "It was supposed to hold off until tonight. Don't worry, I'm a good driver."

"I doubt you'd confess if you were a bad one." She smiled and then sipped her drink.

By the time they arrived at the hospital, a thin layer of snow had blanketed the streets, and the flakes were falling faster. They found parking in the covered garage attached to the hospital and met up with the rest of their boisterous group.

Stan clapped his hands until he had the group's attention. "Everyone, I appreciate that you've donated your time this morning. With the weather turning out as it is, once you've finished your visit and toy deliveries, I'd like you to take the rest of the day off. Go home, and travel safe. If we're closing the office on Monday, I'll let you know on Sunday night."

Emily stifled a sigh. Her car was in the office parking lot. She should have insisted on driving to the hospital herself. Hopefully, the worst of the storm would hold off for another few hours until she eventually made it home.

Damon tugged on his Santa hat, and then reached over and adjusted hers. "There."

She returned his smile and pushed the worry over the drive from her mind. Bringing happiness and smiles to the kids was the only thing that mattered at the moment. She waved to the group and then walked with Damon to the hospital administrator, who would be accompanying them on their visit.

They stopped by the first room, and she recognized Caleb right away. Dark circles under his eyes and worry grooves carved into his face, he looked exhausted. She wasn't sure what she could say to make things better. Losing her grandmother to cancer at the age of ninety was one thing, seeing a little girl no more than five suffering from it was another. Then, her gaze landed on the dark-haired little girl lying in the bed.

The child grinned and waved. "Mr. Damon. You came back."

"Hey, sweetie." He set down his bags and then brought one over to the bed. "This is for you."

"Thanks." She tore through the tissue paper and pulled out a plush pale green turtle. "I love him. Thank you."

"You're welcome." He motioned for Emily to come closer. "This is Miss Emily. She works with me."

"Like Daddy?"

Emily smiled and leaned her hand on Damon's shoulder. "Sort of. Your daddy gets to help make the toys. I get to help Mr. Damon."

Damon's hand covered hers and squeezed. "And like your daddy, she does a good job."

Her throat thickened at the contact and at the words. She cleared her throat and reached into her purse and pulled out the fuzzy white cat. "Gwen, I have a present for you too. I know you have an orange cat that you like. I thought this little guy could keep him company."

Gwen's eyes lit up, and she hugged the toy to her chest. "It's soft. I'll name it Snowy. Here, you can pet him too."

Gwen was such a sweet girl. She would make it. She had to, children were supposed to be enjoying life, not fighting for it. Emily stroked her hand over the soft fur. "I'm glad you like him."

For the next few minutes, she held back tears as

Gwen chattered about everything from schoolwork to hospital procedures to her favorite food from the hospital's menu.

When the hospital administrator prompted they move on, Damon leaned in and gave Gwen a hug. "What do you want for next week? Stickers? A coloring book? More puzzles?"

"Crayons, please."

"You got it." He stood and then shook Caleb's hand. "If you need anything, just say the word."

"Thanks, boss. I'll see you next week."

"Miss Emily?" Gwen's voice stopped her exit from the room.

She turned back. "Yes?"

"Will you come with Mr. Damon next week?"

"Ah…" She glanced at Damon. Would he want her to be there?

"Sure, she will." Eyes twinkling, he slid his arm around Emily's shoulder. He smiled at her and the wistful surge that swirled inside her every time he smiled turned cyclonic spirals. She waved at Gwen and followed Damon into the hall.

They continued the rounds through the decorated floor while snow whirled outside the windows. So many of the children were very, very sick. She wished she could bring their recovery as quickly as handing them a toy. But their tired faces had lit up with excitement when they saw the toys, so hopefully, she had helped in a small way. The kids' joyful reactions, the smiles, the exclamations over the toys, filled her with cheer. She'd expected the kids to be happy, but Damon's response to the kids was the biggest surprise.

He dropped his guard completely with them. Was this what he had been like before his experience with his ex? He'd been in the Army, so surely that had affected him, but this ease he had with the kids made her ache for him.

She knew how deep betrayal could hurt, and how hard moving past it could be. And how scary it was to try to open your heart again.

When they finished their visits, she sent a text to Kira, checking in to see if she and Hunter were also done, while Damon did the same with Aidan. Soon, Damon's phone buzzed with texts from both Hunter and Aidan, just as Kira's response came through on Emily's phone. Minutes later, they all met in the parking garage.

Damon turned to Kira. "What about Mom and Dad?"

"They finished first. Mom called when they were leaving. They're probably halfway home by now."

"Good." He nodded. "Check in when you all get home too. The snow's really coming down."

Craving the warmth from the heated seats, Emily followed Damon to his car. "It's going to be out of your way to drive me back to the office, isn't it?"

"Don't worry about it."

But she did. "I can take the bus or call for a cab."

He shook his head. "No way. It was my idea for us to drive together. I'm not leaving you behind. We'll be fine."

They pulled out of the garage, and the snow was already a few inches thick. Swirling flakes, gray skies, and a windshield that kept fogging up drastically reduced visibility.

The car skidded to the right, but Damon managed to guide it back in the lane. He huffed out a sigh and turned on his hazard lights. "This sucks. I can't see more than ten feet in front of me."

The weather report crackling out of the speakers didn't offer much hope.

They inched along, and minutes ticked by. Caution thickened the air, and they drove without speaking.

Her phone chimed. She pulled it from her purse, expecting to see a text from her sisters or parents. Instead, Paul's name appeared on the screen.

Paul: Come on, Em. Help me out. Give me something on Kallis.

Ugh.

No. Freaking. Way.

She banged out her reply.

Emily: Stop contacting me.

Then she sent a message to her sisters and parents, letting them know she was safe, so they wouldn't worry.

To take her mind off Paul, Emily twisted toward Damon. "Do you stop by and see Gwen every week?"

"As often as I can. If I don't get there, then my parents or someone else from the company stops by."

"That's awfully sweet of you guys."

"She's a great kid." He shrugged. "And it's the right thing to do."

After another hour, two near-accidents and another spin-out, Damon shook his head. "This is crazy. It's too dangerous out here."

Emily bit her lip and squinted into the relentlessly falling white flakes. "We're nowhere near the office."

"But we are near my apartment." He raised a questioning eyebrow at her. "What do you say?"

They weren't safe out on the roads and she didn't want to put either of them in any more danger. Heat flushed through her system at idea of being with Damon for the duration of the storm. "It would be safer to head there. But what if I can't get back to my car later? The snow is getting worse, not better."

"Then you can stay with me." He hit the gas and had to immediately break again. They jerked forward and back roughly. "Look—no expectations. I swear. This storm is already really bad, and if we somehow manage to make it to your car in one piece, you can't be white-knuckling your way home for who knows how long in this mess. I can't take that chance with you."

The concern in his voice and the worry tightening his features showed how much he cared. It was more than she'd expected to see, and the knowledge of it warmed her completely. "And I'd worry about you driving all the way back in this, too. I'd feel awful if something happened."

A smile eased the tension from his face. "So, that's a *yes* for going to my place?"

Craving more of a connection, she rested her hand on his thigh. "It's a yes."

CHAPTER NINE

Damon guided the car through thickening, slippery snow and into his building's first-floor parking garage. As soon as he put the car in park, relief flooded his system. The roads had been terrible. No way did he want to chance getting into an accident with Emily in the car.

His phone buzzed, and he pulled it from his pocket. Two texts from Hunter, one from Aidan, and one from his dad. "Looks like everyone made it home safe."

"Thank goodness." Emily pushed open her door, and frigid air flowed into the car. Shivering, she pulled her scarf up higher. "I hate leaving the warm seats."

"As soon as we get upstairs, I'll warm you up." He had coffee and blankets and himself to offer to her.

Her eyes sparkled when she smiled. "Promise?"

"Whatever you want."

His apartment was on the third floor of the converted warehouse. Oversized windows let in a ton of light and gave them a great view of the swirling storm. The snow was so heavy, all they could see was the blanket of white covering the large evergreens.

He took Emily's coat and hung it with his on the hook by the door.

Her boots clicked on the wooden floor as she traipsed through the living room. "I like your place."

"Thanks." It was still a little sparse on furniture. He hadn't replaced much of what Ursula had stolen. Hadn't wanted to deal with the expense or the hassle. Not when trying to track her down had cost him a considerable amount of time and money.

He shook away the thought.

Ursula didn't matter.

Emily did.

She stood in his living room, arms wrapped around her torso. And shit—were her teeth chattering? His protective instincts kicked into overdrive. "You're freezing."

"Maybe a little. But it's okay."

No. It wasn't.

He bumped up the temperature on the thermostat then crossed to her and pulled her into his arms. She snuggled against his chest, and he felt the tremble move through her before her arms slipped around his waist.

She tilted her head until she met his gaze. "You're like a furnace."

"Any time you need to heat up, I'm here."

"I'll keep that in mind." She pressed a kiss to his chin.

Warmth flowed through his blood. Damon lowered his head, following that lush mouth until it met his—at first light and teasing, and then deeper and harder as passion grew. He banded his arms around her, holding on as the moment solidified into a memory.

After a while, he pulled back. "Come on, let's get you warmed up."

"I thought that was what we were doing." She smiled and brushed her fingers over his cheek. He loved the way her hands felt on his skin.

"It is, but you should have something warm to drink. Or I can make soup. We missed lunch." He led her to the kitchen. "I have coffee, Irish breakfast tea, water, and beer. Or if you want a real drink, I'm pretty well stocked there too."

The liquor bottles on the side counter hadn't been touched in a while. He didn't drink much at home, and if the guys came over, they usually wanted a beer.

"Coffee would be great. And I wouldn't turn down soup either."

He made both, and they ate at the breakfast bar. Steaming bowls of clam chowder and an enormous mug of coffee helped chase away the chill.

He liked seeing her in his space. Sharing the simple meal felt incredibly intimate.

She helped him clean up afterward. As they dried dishes, she asked, "How long have you lived here?"

"A few years now." He knew it didn't look like it. "I was saving for a house for a while, but a few things came up. Never thought I'd still be renting at my age."

"That doesn't matter. My dad keeps saying that once he and my mom retire, they're going back to renting. That way, any house headaches are someone else's problem. Owning or not owning a house isn't a measure of success."

Her words helped. "I remember Kira going to your housewarming party. How long ago was that?"

"Last year. I love the house. It's small, but as soon as I saw it, I knew it was meant to be mine."

"Yeah?" He'd never had that. Never had a place grab him and suck him in. Never had a place that had felt like home.

"But I rented for a long time too." She smiled and topped off their coffees. "As long as you're lucky enough to have a place to live, that's all that matters."

He drank deep while her words settled over him. She was nonjudgmental and caring, and sharing more of himself felt right. "Want a tour?"

"Sure."

He led the way to the hall. "You've seen the living room and kitchen. The bathroom is right here." He pointed to a door on the left. "And this is my bedroom." He nudged the door open with his foot. Thankfully, he'd remembered to make the bed that morning.

She stepped in front of him, and he tried to see it through her eyes. White walls. An old dresser from his parents' house. The wide bed with the iron headboard and gray bedspread. The black curtains that kept his room as dark as possible from the bright safety lights out in the courtyard. His hockey stick and equipment bag in one corner. But Emily's presence out-shined everything. He could picture them tangled together on the bed, or pressed up against the wall, or sweeter moments too, like bringing her a cup of coffee early in the morning.

Her eyes were warm as she turned to face him. "It suits you."

"So do you." The words were out before they'd even registered in his brain. But before he could even begin to figure out how to call them back, she placed her free hand on his chest, and her smile increased until it was wide enough to brighten up the room.

"I'm glad." She pressed a kiss to his cheek, but then stepped back and moved into the hall before he could turn it into more.

He followed and opened the door to the other bedroom. This room was special. It housed boxes of hockey, baseball, and football cards, display cases of autographed pucks and helmets, signed hockey sticks, and three framed jerseys on the wall.

Emily walked to the center of the room and turned in a slow circle. Tension tightened his muscles, and he braced for her derision, but her eyes lit up, and a smile bloomed across her face. "This is so cool."

Surprise mixed with disbelief as he gaped at her. "Really?"

"My dad would be so jealous. He's collected cards for years. I sometimes go with him to the memorabilia conventions. We've spent hours waiting in line for auto-graphs, or hunting down cards so that he could complete a set." She sounded like she didn't think it was a stupid hobby at all. Instead, she wandered over to the boxes, smiling as she inspected them. "So, what's your favorite?"

"Uh..." *Unreal* that she'd react like this. He couldn't believe it. "I guess my favorite piece is the signed hockey stick from Colin Fraser. He was the team captain when the Bedlam won the Cup back when I was a kid."

"Nice. My dad has his rookie card." She picked up and then put down pucks and peeked in boxes. "You have a great collection."

"This is nothing. I used to have a lot more."

Her brows lifted and then she laid her hand on his shoulder, sympathy in her gaze. "Kira mentioned that your ex-girlfriend walked out with a lot of your things. Including some of these."

"She thought it was a stupid hobby. Told me I needed to grow up." His anger and resentment grew as his focus landed on the empty spaces where his most prized cards used to be. "Said it often enough that I felt like maybe I *should* give it up. She sucked all the fun out of it. Convinced me to sell my vintage Guy Proch hockey card and a few other things. Claimed the money would be better used for a down payment on a house rather than sitting in a box. And less than a month later, she was gone, taking the card sets that were worth the most money, and half the contents of the apartment and my bank account with her."

"Oh, Damon. I'm so sorry." Emily's hand rubbed up

and down his back. Soothing strokes, but he couldn't relax.

He'd been an idiot to fall for Ursula and to be swayed by her lies. And he'd never been able to track her down. She'd slipped out of town just as quietly as she'd arrived. The two investigators he'd hired hadn't turned up anything. Most likely, she was a con artist who'd lied about her identity and had already moved on to her next victim.

Emily's hand continued to knead his muscles. "You know, a few big card shows are coming up, one in January and another in March. You should come with my dad and me."

Bitterness didn't help anything. He shook his head to clear his thoughts and focus on the woman in front of him. "You really like going with him?"

"I have the best time. He gets so excited, it's like Christmas morning or something."

"You don't think it's silly?"

"His collecting cards and memorabilia? No way. It makes him happy. That's all that matters."

Her supportive stance soothed the sore spot that still stung from Ursula's condescending comments. He leaned into her hand. "What do you like about it?"

"Meeting the old-time players is always fun. And hanging out with my dad is the best. We didn't spend a lot of time together while I was growing up because he worked two jobs. So getting to share in a hobby now is special." She pulled her phone from her pocket and swiped her finger across the screen a few times, then held it out to him. "This is what I'm getting him for Christmas."

The photo on the screen of the vintage football card sent dual shards of envy and surprise through him. "Whoa. How the hell did you score that?"

"I always make friends with the dealers, and they keep an eye out for what I need. I'm picking this one up from the shop on Front Street next week."

"I've been in there a few times." To sell, to buy, and to chat about cards with the pros who shared his passion.

"You and my dad would hit it off. He loves talking about his collection. You really should come with us to those shows."

He cupped her shoulders in his hands. "Thanks for the offer. I'd like that."

"Then it's a date." She rose onto her toes and kissed him, softly, slowly, and sweetly.

The wind whistled and howled and rattled the windows. Emily eased away from him, slipped her phone into her pocket, and then crossed to the window. "It's really coming down out there."

"Let's get the official weather update." He closed the bedroom door behind them and then turned on the TV in the living room. On screen, Paul Redmond from Channel 10 gave a report, filling in for the regular anchor. Emily grimaced and then glared at the screen.

Damon raised his brow. "You don't like him?"

"He's my ex."

Her stiff posture and tightly spoken words drew out

his protective side. He moved closer to her. "The guy who lied about your work?"

"Yeah."

"I don't like him either. He was a pompous ass when the recall happened." He flipped channels until he found another weather report. "He started pestering me with phone calls and emails a few days ago too. I forwarded the calls to our PR team. Let them handle him."

"I guess he wasn't satisfied with that because he sent me a text while we were driving here."

His muscles stiffened, and his stomach clenched. "I didn't realize you guys still spoke."

"We don't. I ran into him a few weeks ago, when I was at the hotel doing the gala checklist. He saw my business card and found out I worked for you. But other than that, and today's message, I hadn't heard from him since I broke things off and left my old job."

"Oh." He kept his voice casual, even though his internal alert signal was going off like an air horn. "You said he must not have been satisfied. Does that mean he asked you about the recall?"

"And the prototype. He wants information."

Shit. Shit. Shit.

She laid her hand on his shoulder. "I told him to stop contacting me. But I have to tell you, he can be relentless, so just because you push him off to PR doesn't mean he'll stop trying to contact you. Or anyone else with contact info readily available. You might want to talk to your parents and let everyone know, so he doesn't catch them off-guard."

"I'll do that."

"Good." Her arms wrapped around his torso and she leaned into his back. Where the hell had this woman been hiding all his life? Oh yeah, that was right—in plain sight.

He clasped his hand over the one resting on his chest and soaked up her support. He didn't want to think about Paul anymore. "So, the storm is worse than they thought because of the lake effect snow."

"As long as it doesn't dump six feet at once, like it did a few years ago." She shivered and sighed and then slipped around him to lean against his side. "That wasn't fun at all."

"Yeah, it sucked." He groaned at the expected total. "Still, three feet isn't going to be any fun either."

"Three?" Her mouth dropped open, and she squinted at the TV. "They're closing the roads soon to everyone except essential personnel. How am I going to get home?"

"You can stay here." He was all for the idea of her spending the night.

"I don't have any of my things."

"I'm sure I can find a spare toothbrush." But he knew what she meant. "There's a grocery store three blocks away. I can walk down and pick up what you need."

"I couldn't ask you to do that—not alone anyway. If you're going to brave the cold and snow, I will too."

"You should stay here."

"Damon." She placed her hands on her hips, facing

off against him. "I appreciate it, but I'm not going to let you run out there while I stay snuggled and warm. I'm coming too."

"You're stubborn."

"Well, I've spent the last few weeks learning from the best."

He couldn't stop his lips from twitching. "All right. Then let's go."

They bundled into coats and hats and gloves. Then he noticed the skinny heels of her boots. "You're going to be okay trekking through ice and snow in those?"

Her eyes flashed a warning. "They'll be fine."

"All right." He'd just make sure to keep his arm around her.

The trip took much longer than usual. Wind whistled through the frosty air and snow swirled and fell at a relentless pace. Rather than walking in a winter wonderland, the storm was more like walking through a snow globe on steroids. Damon kept his head down and his arm around Emily.

She picked up a bunch of travel-sized items, and he loaded a basket with more cans of soup.

The return trip was worse. They waded through snow nearly a foot deep as giant flakes soaked through their hats and the cold numbed his fingers.

Emily's lips were blue when they finally stumbled back into his apartment. He tugged off his dripping outerwear and hung it over one of the barstools. "You should take a hot shower."

"Can I borrow something to change into?"

The thought of her wearing something of his was enough to make his insides simmer. "Sure."

He directed her to the bathroom and set out some towels, then dug through his dresser until he found a pair of fleece pants with a drawstring at the waist and the softest sweatshirt he owned. After adding wool socks to the pile, he knocked on the bathroom door. The shower was running. He knocked harder and cracked the door open. "Em?"

"In the shower."

He nudged it open wider. "I'm going to leave clothes on the sink."

"Oh. Thank you."

The steam filling the room added fuel to his fantasy. He laid the clothes down and left before he could do something they both might not be ready for.

After changing his clothes, he sent texts to Aidan and Hunter, reminding them of that six-feet-of-snow-storm that had blanketed the region. He and Hunter had been at Aidan's house, and the three of them had ridden out the worst of the days together.

Emily emerged from the bathroom, hair twisted up into a knot, smelling like his soap, and looking far too sexy in his clothes. "Thank you. That helped."

He rose and held his arm out, pleased when she slipped under it and wrapped her arm around his waist. "Hungry?"

"Starving."

"Frozen pizza, more soup, or pasta?"

She grinned at him. "I'm Italian. Pasta is always the right answer."

"I have a package of fettuccine in the fridge." He linked their fingers together and drew her to the kitchen. "Tell me you don't make your own."

"I've only done it a few times. My grandmother always made it from scratch. Every Sunday, she'd have the whole family over for dinner and homemade pasta was always on the menu. But I'm fine with store-bought fresh or boxed." She watched while he took it out, then grabbed a pot and filled it with water. "As long as it's cooked *al dente* and we have tomato sauce."

"I always over-cook it, so I'll leave that to you. But yeah, I have a jar of sauce." He handed her the jar of marinara.

She studied the back of the label and then dumped half the contents into a small pot. "Sauce is one of the things I do like to make from scratch."

"You make your own?" He was impressed.

She shrugged as she worked. "It reminds me of my grandmother, and it's relaxing. Maybe you could come over for dinner sometime, and I'll make it for you."

"I'd like that." He slid his hand across her shoulders. She rarely wore her hair pulled back. Piled high as it was, it gave him a great view of her long neck. He couldn't resist stroking the exposed skin.

She shivered and leaned into his hands. His lips followed the path his fingers had taken, and he slid his arms around her waist. Her hands clamped onto his arms, holding him close.

Steam billowed out of the covered pot on the stove. With a sigh, Damon lowered his arms and stepped back. Emily dropped the pasta into the water. "Fresh takes a lot less time to cook." She stirred it and set the timer.

He knew better than to start touching her again. After grabbing plates and forks, he took two beers from the fridge and set everything on the bar.

The pasta was the best he'd ever eaten, although he was sure that had more to do with the company than the actual noodles.

When they'd finished eating, they moved to the couch, and he flipped through channels until she made a sound of interest at an old action movie.

Sliding his arm around her shoulder felt as natural as breathing. Her body snuggling closer felt as if she were meant for him.

Maybe she was.

He'd been angry for so long, and then lonely for so long. But Emily had been the first woman to make him want to lower the guards around his heart.

Maybe it was time to finally take that chance.

CHAPTER TEN

Emily stifled a yawn and glanced out the window. The glow from two streetlights showed the snow continuing to fall. Just looking at it made her shiver, and she tugged the sleeves of her borrowed sweatshirt over her hands.

"Still cold?" Damon rubbed his hands along her arms.

"Not when I'm next to you." She leaned her head against the back of the couch and looked at him. He made her happy, went out of his way to take care of her, and she was so attracted to him... holding back didn't make sense anymore.

She brushed her fingers over his cheek and then lifted her face to his. Folding her fingers around his neck, she exerted just enough pressure to nudge him down to meet her lips.

Warm and firm, they settled over hers and then he took control, slanting his mouth as his tongue teased and tasted hers.

He leaned over her, pressing her deeper into the cushions as his hand slid along her thigh. Back and forth, back and forth, stoking her need higher.

"Damon." She grabbed a handful of his shirt and tugged him against her.

He groaned long and low and shifted until she lay under him, and then his hot fingers stroked the exposed skin where her shirt had ridden high.

She pressed into his touch and let her hands wander across his back, exploring his muscles.

He kissed a path down her neck and tugged her shirt collar away to lay another row of kisses across her collarbone.

She sighed, weaving her fingers through his hair.

He reversed the trail, and when his lips closed over hers again, his hand roamed higher and his fingers closed over her breast. She sighed into his mouth and tugged at his shirt, wanting the barrier removed. On a groan, he leaned back and pulled his shirt over his head and tossed it to the floor.

Her eyes widened at his muscles. Hard and defined, they showed the effort he put into running and playing hockey.

Damon fingered the edge of her shirt and quirked his brow. Goose bumps dotted her skin and she nodded and sat up and helped him slip it over her head. She glanced at her plain black bra, wishing it were sexier, but then Damon reached for her and pulled her to standing, and the worry over the bra faded away under the intensity of his gaze.

He drew her to him and splayed his fingers over the back of her head, then bent until their lips met again. Sweet and sexy, the kisses were more potent than wine. She traced his pecs and then the six-pack of his abs. Those muscles sucked in at her exploration, and his hands became rough, streaking across her skin as though he were desperate to touch every inch of her body. Fingers caressed then became more insistent, kneading her breasts while flicking his thumb over the hard tips of her pebbled nipples. His lips grazed along her neck and sucked up a mark in the sensitive spot where her neck met her shoulder.

She arched into him and then moaned as his arousal ground against her stomach.

Reaching around, she unclasped her bra and shook it to the floor. Damon's eyes glittered, and he gathered her close once more.

The feeling of his hot skin pressing into her flesh sent her desire soaring. She poured her feelings into their next kiss.

He untied the drawstring at her waist. Emily shifted off of him and the soft fleece pants fell to the floor. Shivering as the air hit her skin, she stepped out of the pile of clothes.

She smiled at Damon's focus on her underwear. Her red and green striped pair edged in red lace rode low on her hips.

His hands clamped on her waist. "It's like a Christmas present."

Emily traced a finger over the bulge in his pants. "Maybe you should unwrap it."

Those hot hands tightened at her words, and she moaned at his strength. Freeing him from his sweats took far longer than it should have thanks to his seeking hands wreaking havoc on her concentration. Finally, she managed to push them down, and he kicked free.

Gray boxer briefs hugged his body, displaying his erection and powerful thighs. She slipped her fingers into his waistband. "I'm thinking you need more festive underwear."

And then he nudged a finger under the lace she wore, teased it along her folds, then entered her, and as pleasure bloomed she wasn't thinking at all.

He shifted them until her body leaned against the wall and continued to devour her with lips and teeth and hands. When he paused to bring his lips back to hers, she took him in her hands, seeking to drive him as crazy as he'd driven her. Slow, deliberate strokes while she watched his eyes close and his head fall forward until it rested on the cool wall over her shoulder. Then faster, tighter strokes while he groaned and muttered curses, and his long, low moan vibrated in the air and feathered over her skin.

Lightning-quick, his hand gripped her thigh and tugged it over his. That bump and grind began again, growing faster and faster as his cock rubbed her in all the right places. She dug her nails into his shoulder, desperate to feel him inside of her. "Damon."

Teasing the head of his cock over her clit, he spoke

between pants. "I want you so bad. To be so deep inside you, to feel you tight around me."

"I have a condom in my purse." It had been in there for months, forgotten, in an inner pouch, until she'd found it the other day while searching for her lip gloss.

"There's a few in the end table drawer. They've been in there so long they might be expired. I'll check." He nipped her lips, then stepped away and retrieved a foil packet from a box in the end table by the couch. "They're still good."

He rolled it on, then stooped a little lower, lining up with her entrance, and with his gaze locked with hers, he thrust inside. Her breath caught, and she dug her nails into his shoulder.

His hips set a rhythm, snapping over and over while she rode the waves of pleasure—building, building—until she crested, surfing the tidal wave all the way to the last delicious crash. With a final surge, he ground his hips into hers and then groaned out his release.

For a long moment, they held each other while they gasped for breath. And then Damon lifted his head and met her gaze. Smiling, he brushed her hair from her face, and his lips met hers in a kiss that was deep and slow and sexy.

After a while, cold prickled fresh goose bumps on her skin, and she eased away, untangling their limbs. "It's getting cold."

"Want to share a shower? Then we can warm up in bed." He pulled her toward the bathroom without waiting for an answer. She gratefully followed. Soon, steam filled the room.

The hot spray of the water felt good on her skin and Damon felt even better as they took turns soaping each other up.

Then, they climbed into bed, and he wrapped his arm around her, spent and ready to rest. And contentment like she'd never known lulled her to sleep.

Emily woke to a darkened room. Sunlight peeked through the edges of the curtains, but not enough for her to hazard a guess on the hour of the day. Damon's skin was warm against her back, and his arm banded around her. She snuggled deeper into the blankets.

He pressed a soft kiss to her shoulder. "Morning."

She twisted until she could see his face. "Do you think it's still snowing?"

"It wasn't supposed to stop until this afternoon or tonight." He nuzzled her neck and the hand resting on her stomach began to stroke. "You feel good."

Her pulse scrambled, and her nerve endings went on alert. So hyper-sensitive. She could feel him everywhere.

He brushed his finger across her lips. "I'll make coffee. You wait here where it's warm. I'll bring it in."

She rolled until she faced him. "I always start with a glass of water first." It was one of the health tips her grandmother had sworn by. Some days, she really missed her. Grandma Emily would've loved to hear about Damon. She lifted her arm to look at her bracelet. It wasn't there. And she didn't remember taking it off.

Tossing the blankets aside, she rose and pulled the pillows off the bed, then tugged the sheet and blankets to the edge of the mattress.

"What's going on?" Brow creasing, Damon sat up.

"My bracelet. It must have fallen off."

He climbed out of bed and tugged on a pair of sweats. "What does it look like?"

"It's gold, with a thin chain and a small plate with Emily written across it."

"I remember seeing you wear it."

She'd worn it a lot during her first two weeks at the company. "It was my grandmother's. Her mom gave it to her for her sixteenth birthday, and she gave it to me on mine."

Her most favorite and treasured piece of jewelry.

She searched the floor, then went into the living room. After shaking out the shirt she'd borrowed from Damon the day before, she tugged it over her chilled skin.

"Here." He tossed her the fleece pants, then went into the kitchen and shook out the clothes she'd worn in the snow. "It's not here."

"I can't lose it." She paced the room, gaze wandering back and forth, scanning for the bracelet.

"When is the last time you remember seeing it on your wrist?"

"When I washed my hands in the restroom at work

yesterday morning. I didn't realize it was gone because my sweater covered it." She wrapped her arms around her middle. "It could be anywhere. The office. The office parking lot. Your car. The coffee shop. The hospital. The parking garage. The grocery store. Any sidewalk we were on."

Outside the window, snowflakes still fell. She glared at them. "And with all the snow covering everything, and plows moving piles around, it could be gone for good."

Damon slid his arm around her shoulders. "I'll call Ben and ask him to check the coffee shop. We'll call the hospital too. And we can search my car. I'll retrace our steps to the grocery store if I have to. And we can check the office on Monday."

"I have to find it. That's the only keepsake I have of hers."

"I understand. Come drink your water and coffee, and I'll call Ben."

While Damon spoke with Ben, she guzzled the water and then downed the coffee, all the while berating herself for not realizing the bracelet had fallen off.

Damon joined her and filled his cup with coffee. "The streets are still closed so Ben can't get to the shop, but he'll check as soon as he can."

"If the streets are closed, that means we can't drive to the hospital to look for it. We'll need to call them and see if anyone turned it in. I can't believe I didn't hear it hit the floor or the ground when it fell."

"Maybe it fell on carpeted floor, like my car or the

office." He laid his hand over hers and squeezed. "We'll look everywhere, don't worry."

After a breakfast of eggs and toast, they called the hospital, then checked the hall, stairwell, garage, and car. No luck.

She tugged on her still-wet boots and walked with Damon back to the grocery store. Two additional feet of snow had fallen since their trip the day before. Hoping to find it laying there waiting for her seemed silly but she still had to check. The store was open, but no one had turned in a bracelet. On the way home, she walked in front of Damon, eyes scanning the snow. They reached his building and her hope of discovering the bracelet was fading fast.

A snowball arced over her head, and then one hit the center of her back. She spun around, nearly losing her balance in the three-foot drifts. "What the heck?"

"We're going to find it. But worrying yourself sick won't help." Smiling, Damon palmed more snow into his hand and crushed it into a ball. "A little stress release might help. Come on. Play."

He'd done so much to help her. She drummed up a smile for him. They'd done all they could do as far as searching for today. Cold seeped through her gloves, but she packed together a snowball, knowing she had the world's worst aim. "Keep in mind I'm doing this in heels."

"Yeah, yeah." He tossed the ball, and it hit her right on the thigh.

"You'll pay for that." She winged her attempt at him but he dove to the left, and it sailed over his head.

They kept up the attack, and she managed to score one direct hit and claimed victory. Damon tugged her to him and kissed her in the middle of the sea of white. She was soaked through thanks to their game, but once his lips landed on hers, she didn't care.

When they staggered into his apartment, he pointed her toward the shower. "You know the drill. Get warmed up in there. I'll find new clothes for you."

"Maybe you'll join me too?"

"I like the way you think." He took her coat and then brushed a kiss on her forehead. "We'll keep looking. Don't worry."

"Yeah." But of course, she would worry. Not having that bracelet almost felt like a part of her was missing.

On Sunday morning, the city lifted the driving ban. She and Damon retraced their steps as best they could, driving to the coffee shop and then the hospital. Careful scouring hadn't yielded her bracelet. She was beginning to think she'd never see it again. Searching the office would have to wait until Monday because the plows hadn't yet cleared the parking lot.

Emily stared out the car's window as the streets rolled by. Sadness settled over her like a heavy blanket. In some ways, losing the bracelet was like losing her grandmother all over again. She turned toward Damon.

He'd been amazing, but she didn't want her mood to bring him down. "I should go home. Since we're already on the road, if it's easier, you can drop me off now."

He laid his hand on her knee and squeezed. "You don't have to go."

"I need clothes for tomorrow. I can't show up at the office in your clothes or the ones I wore on Friday." Which were the ones she wore now, although they were clean, thanks to his washer and dryer.

"How about we stop at your place, and you can pack a bag? Since your car is buried under all that snow at the office, we can spend the night together and then drive in to work together tomorrow."

Several of the smaller streets still hadn't been plowed, and the piles of snow dumped in sporadic places meant the commute would be worse than usual. Having to drive out of his way to pick her up in the morning would make things ever more difficult. "Are you sure?"

He slowed the car to a stop at a red light and turned to her. "But if you want to go home and you want some breathing room, that's fine too. I'm fine with driving over tomorrow morning and picking you up."

"I do need to shovel a path in front of my house and clear the snow out of my driveway." She touched his hand, unsure if disappointment was shuttering his gaze. "I'm not brushing you off. That stuff shouldn't wait. It only gets harder to do if you let it go, with the melting and refreezing."

"If you want a hand, I can help. Thanks to living in apartments, I haven't shoveled a driveway in years."

She wasn't ready to say goodbye to him. "Three feet is a lot to move. The least I can do is cook for you."

He raised his brows. "Homemade tomato sauce?"

"I think I can make that happen." She leaned back as the light changed to green. "Both of those things are going to take a while. Maybe you're the one who should pack a bag."

"You're not kidding, are you?"

She shook her head. "The sauce takes a few hours. And my driveway is long. I really should invest in a snow blower."

He turned onto the street for his apartment building. "I'll pack, and then we'll head over and get started."

Having him with her would help keep her mind off of the bracelet, and maybe he needed a break too, from his apartment and the reminders of what his ex had stolen.

Her heart ached to think of someone hurting him that deeply. Falling in love made a person vulnerable. She was falling for Damon. But she was scared to let herself fall all the way.

In case she ended up with her heart broken.

CHAPTER ELEVEN

He hated playing against the Dragons.

Mood dark with the thought of going against the dirtiest players in the league, Damon suited up in the locker room. He hadn't slept well the night before. Staying at Emily's house had meant he was far more interested in her than in catching some shut-eye.

In the five days since the storm had ended, they'd spent the night together three times, twice at her place and once at his. His body was dragging, and that wouldn't help his team. Willing the electrolytes to rally him, he downed half a bottle of a sports drink.

Beside him, Aidan put on his goalie pads. "Skye said that Emily will be here tonight."

"Yeah, I asked her if she wanted to come. She's been so bummed about the missing bracelet. I thought hanging out with Kira and Skye would help." He laced up his skates.

After he and Emily had visited Gwen in the hospital

during lunch, they stopped by the front desk to see if anyone had turned in the bracelet. No matter that the hospital had both their cell numbers, stopping by in person was still a smart move in case something had slipped through the cracks. The fact that no one had yet turned in the bracelet had cast a cloud over Emily's spirits. With each day that passed, she appeared to lose more hope that it would be found.

"You picked a great match-up. The Dragons hate us as much as we hate them. I hope she doesn't mind a physical game."

Hunter lumbered over to their spot, smoothing the tape on his stick. "I heard *hate*. You must be talking about Waverly."

Damon stood and rolled his shoulders. Annoyance flared at the thought of the most-hated player on the opposing team. An annoyance that every member of his team shared, especially Hunter. "Not specifically by name, but yeah, he's mostly the reason for the hate. Hunter, try not to get tossed from the game tonight."

"Hey, I can't help it if he starts something."

"Dude, he *always* starts something."

"And I'm happy to finish it."

Aidan tossed his glove at Hunter. "We know. You're leading our team in penalty minutes, mostly thanks to fighting with him."

"Come on, let's get out there." Damon signaled to the team, and they trooped to the ice.

Spotting Emily in the first row with Kira and Skye, he waved when he caught her gaze. Seeing her there gave him the energy boost he needed. In a way, he and she were a team, united against Paul, united in searching for her bracelet. He liked that idea a lot.

He lined up for the opening face-off—thankfully not against Waverly—confident with Hunter on defense and Aidan minding the net. He won it, knocked the puck to his line mate, Ben, and skated down the ice. One of the Dragons barreled into the left-winger with an elbow to his face, sending him right into the boards. Ben slowly got to his feet, and the ref sent the Dragon player to the penalty box.

Right then, Damon knew the game would be no different from any other game against the Dragons, except they usually didn't start the cheap shots so early.

Play resumed and descended into grabbing and tripping and elbowing and boarding. Both teams had guys in the penalty box more that they were out of it. He'd never played in a game that was almost a constant short-handed or power-play situation.

For two and a half periods, he managed to keep his cool. Scoring a goal off of an assist from Ben helped.

The game was tied when he battled Waverly along the boards for control of the puck. One of his teammates swooped in and managed to knock the puck away and sent it flying toward the Dragon's zone. Damon turned to follow the play, and Waverly's stick slammed down in a slash across his forearms. The pain and motion forced him to drop his own stick and lose one of his gloves. Seething, he whipped around. "What the fucking hell, asshole."

Smirking, Waverly raised his hands in the air and skated backward a step. "What do you mean? I didn't do anything."

"No? You got a body double I don't know about?" Damon dropped his other glove, advanced on Waverly, and threw a right hook. The idiot's head snapped back, and Damon grabbed hold of the jerk's jersey to keep him close. Throwing two quick jabs, he hit as hard as the pain radiating down his arm would allow.

The ref zoomed over and pulled Damon back. "Enough. That's it. You're done, Kallis."

Damon tugged away from his grasp. "You serious? He fucking slashed me."

"All I saw was you going after him. You're done. Be glad it's a five-minute major and not anything more."

Pissed off, Damon skated toward the bench. His teammates, both on the ice and on the bench, were yelling at the ref for missing the call and at Waverly for taking the cheap shot, and then hollering encouragement and reassurances to Damon.

Hunter tapped him as he passed. "Don't worry, D. We'll get him back."

He smashed his stick against the boards. It snapped in two. Leaving the remnants where they were, he skated off the ice. Anger carried him in fast steps to the locker room.

He pulled off his uniform and equipment and shoved it all into his bag. Muscles tense, blood burning, he couldn't calm down. The shower he took didn't help. He leaned his face into the water, plotting ways to get even the next time the Blades played the Dragons.

"Damon?" Emily's voice called from the locker room.

"Hold on." He turned off the spray, then grabbed a towel and dried off fast. Two minutes later, towel slung around his waist, he headed back into the locker room.

Her eyes widened, and her gaze roamed over his body. "I wanted to see how you were. Did he hurt you?"

The long red mark on his forearm was tender to the touch and his fist was sore, but he didn't think anything was broken. "I'm fine."

"Let me see." Her breath sucked in, and she traced her fingers over the discolored skin. "I saw him hit you. I wanted to get out there and hit him back."

"I appreciate that." He wrapped his other hand around her hip and tugged her against him. "I appreciate you coming to check on me even more."

Her fingers slid into his hair, and her body lined up with his just right. "I'll tell you a secret, I was checking you out the entire game."

He groaned, tightening his hold. "Did you like what you saw?"

"So much." Her whisper ghosted over his cheek. "You looked pretty hot out there."

All his energy and aggression from the game channeled into desperation for her. He backed her against the lockers and tugged at her sweater until his hands found the soft, warm skin of her torso.

Her hands skimmed over his chest, then one

threaded in his hair, and the other slid down his stomach, making him suck in a breath as she traced a path along the towel's edge.

He crashed his lips into hers and slipped his hands to her back, pulling her in even as he pressed closer. Unable to get close enough, impatient with the barriers between them, he rocked his hips, spurred on when she mimicked his motions.

She was everything. Soft, hot, sexy, intoxicating, and he wanted to lose himself in her.

The sounds of someone trudging closer and grumbling echoed from the hall, growing ever louder. With a sigh, Damon lifted his head and looked at the doorway.

Hunter strode in with a thunderous expression darkening his face. He stopped short when his gaze landed on Emily. "Oh. Hey."

Damon smoothed Emily's shirt, keeping her close while his gaze zeroed in on his friend, checking for injuries. "Why aren't you on the ice or the bench?"

"I hit him and got tossed."

"Waverly?"

"Yeah. He tripped me, so I let him have it, hard enough for both you and me."

Uh-oh. An angry Hunter was never a good thing. Damon groaned. "How many times did you hit him?"

"Two or ten." He shrugged and then grinned. "Lost count. He had it coming."

"Did he get tossed too?"

"Yeah. And the ref gave him two minutes for tripping. Ben just scored on the power play. We're up by one. Seven minutes to go."

"Awesome." He pulled Emily closer.

She lightly pushed against his chest. "I should go. Let you get dressed, and Hunter get changed."

He shot Hunter a look and his friend seemed to receive the message. Hunter backed up toward the door. "No worries, Emily. I'll, uh, go hang out with the Zamboni driver and watch the rest of the game."

When he left, Damon slipped his hands under her shirt. "Now, where were we?"

"We only have seven minutes. That isn't a long time."

"Not long enough for all I want to do, but long enough for this." The rush of adrenaline had faded. He cupped her face in his hands. Glancing from her eyes to her mouth and back again, he leaned in, sinking slowly into the kiss. His ex hadn't ever gone to a game. Until now, he hadn't realized how much that had bothered him.

Her hand rested over his heart. Could she feel how it beat harder when he held her?

Time was ticking away. The last thing he needed was his teammates barreling in and finding them tangled around each other. He broke the kiss and traced the side of her face with his finger. "Thanks for being here tonight."

"I had fun. But if that guy puts his hands on you again, Kira and Skye will have to hold me back from climbing over the boards." She pressed a kiss to the slash on his arm. "Now I better get out of here before your teammates come in."

He watched her walk away, then finished getting dressed. In the distance, the horn sounded, ending the game, followed by his teammates erupting in cheers.

Moments later, his teammates filed into the room, talking about their win and voicing complaints against the other team. Damon made plans to meet most of the guys at the pub for a victory drink. He couldn't wait to celebrate and introduce Emily to his teammates.

But he could wait until Hunter was ready. His friend tended to move slower than the other guys. After every game, either he or Aidan waited while Hunter finished showering and dressing, in case he needed help moving around and just keeping him company so he didn't worry about always being the last one out. His friends had always had his back, and he would forever return that favor.

Finally, they met up with Emily, Kira, and Skye. Fresh energy filled him as his gaze connected with Emily. His heart skipped a beat at the way she smiled at him. Shouldering his bag, he wrapped his other arm around her shoulders. "Ready to go?"

She snuggled into his side. "Let's celebrate your win."

Like every other place in town, the pub was decked out with strands of twinkling lights and garland. Rock and pop versions of Christmas songs echoed from the speakers.

Chatting with his teammates and friends, Damon nursed a beer and kept his arm around Emily. Having her there made the celebration all the more special. He wanted this—wanted her—with him. Hockey games, evenings out with friends, cozy days with just the two of them, all if it… in his life in a significant way.

As the conversation turned to everyone's plans for the holiday, the desire to share part of the holiday with her grew so strong he couldn't wait to ask. Brushing his hand along her arm, he nestled in closer. "I know you mentioned you were getting together with a lot of your family, but do you think you'll have any free time Christmas Eve or Christmas Day so we could see each other?"

She twisted toward him. "We have a huge family and friends open house and dinner at my parents' place on Christmas Eve. If you're not doing anything then, you're welcome to come and join us."

"Sure." Pleasure warmed him better than the alcohol. He liked that she was letting him in. "Maybe you'll come back home with me afterward? We can wake up together on Christmas morning."

"I like that idea. And I don't have any plans for Christmas Day, so we can relax and have a late, indulgent breakfast." Her lips pursed and she tilted her head. "You don't have any decorations at your place."

True, his place was pretty bare on the decorating front. Unlike Emily's home. Her place was all light colors—whites, grays, and creams, with accents and touches that made every inch seem well-loved. And every room was decorated for Christmas. She had a small artificial tree with white lights and crystal ornaments in her living room, cinnamon-scented candles everywhere, wreaths, garland, and bowls of ornaments adorning various surfaces. Even her bathrooms and kitchen were decorated with snowman towels and seasonal-scented soap. "I can buy some decorations for my place, but it still wouldn't be a nice and inviting and as Christmas-in-every-room like you have."

She walked her fingers up his chest, then traced a pattern over his heart. "How about you come back home with me that night?"

"I like that idea." He could picture a fire crackling in the fireplace, the lights twinkling on the tree, and Emily beside him, soft and warm. Or making their own heat in her sleigh bed that was as soft as snow.

Picturing the bed, he wanted to be back there. He tugged her closer. "Want some company tonight?"

"I'd love some."

Ben clapped him on the shoulder and set his glass on the bar with a *clink*. "Did you guys find that bracelet yet?"

"No." Emily's answer was soft and full of sorrow.

"Don't be discouraged. The snow's going to take a while to fully melt. Maybe it'll turn up after that. Just in case, I put a sign up at the coffee shop and have been checking the parking lot every day too."

"Thanks, bud." Damon nodded at his friend. "We appreciate it."

"Anytime. I'm heading out. See you at the next game."

Damon waved and tucked Emily against his side once again. When they got back to her place, he'd do whatever it took to put a smile on her face. He didn't like seeing her upset, and he was frustrated the bracelet hadn't turned up. If it were gone forever, she would be devastated.

He needed to fix it.

Somehow.

CHAPTER TWELVE

Frustration pulsed with every beat of his heart. Gripping the cell phone tight to his ear, Damon glared at the Saturday afternoon sunlight streaming through the windows as he paced the length of his living room and listened to his lead engineer's status report. The latest prototype of the toy had hit a snag. Caleb and the design team were putting in overtime, trying to correct the flaw. Catching the problem now rather than later was better, but anything that slowed progress was frustrating.

He ended the call with Caleb, then swore.

"Problems?" Hunter set down his beer and stretched back out on the couch, legs propped up on the coffee table.

"They're still trying to correct the issue. I don't know how they missed it on the earlier designs."

"Do you have the plans here? Pull them up."

He did, thanks to Emily putting them in the storage

cloud. Grabbing his laptop off the breakfast bar, he also swiped his coffee and then joined Hunter.

Aidan came out of the kitchen, holding a mug of decaf, and sat on his other side. "Is the problem with the mechanics, the materials, or the program?"

"Caleb said there's a delay with reaction time and he's not sure what's causing it. It also seems a little top-heavy now. Something's off with the weight of the materials."

They reviewed the designs and plans and tossed ideas back and forth, and then sent the engineer a list of questions and suggestions.

With a sigh, Damon closed his computer and set it on the coffee table. "I guess that's enough for now. I don't want to bug them, and I know we need to give them time to work things out."

Hunter nudged his arm. "Can't wait until this one is released, can you?"

"The recall is all I think about."

"I'd believe that if I hadn't seen you with Emily. You're thinking of her at least fifty percent of the time."

Maybe he was. He'd spent the last few days calling every vintage jewelry shop in Western New York, and every online shop he could find. No one had a bracelet that could double as a replacement for Emily's. He'd wracked his brain trying to come up with a meaningful Christmas present for her, and a replacement bracelet had seemed the perfect solution. "I still haven't had any luck with the bracelet, and I've run out of stores to contact."

"Why not go into the local shops and look for your-self?" Aidan met his gaze over the rim of his mug. "You're relying on people to check for you, and you know as well as I do that people overlook things all the time."

"He's right." Hunter nodded. "I see that in IT every day."

"My time's limited. I wanted to keep it a surprise from Emily. I've had a hard enough time finding excuses to go out of the office and make calls during the day."

"So, let's go now." Aidan's simple suggestion surprised him.

"You really want to spend the afternoon going to jewelry stores?" He shook his head in disbelief. It hadn't been just the three of them in a long while. He knew they were looking forward to hanging out as much as he. No way could he ask them to give up the after-noon that way.

Aidan and Hunter traded glances, and then both of them shrugged.

"It's important to you." Aidan drained his coffee mug and then rose.

Hunter clicked off the TV and slowly stood. "You'd do it for us."

And this was why he loved his friends. They'd kick his ass if he needed it, but they always provided uncon-ditional support. "Thanks."

Hunter shrugged into his coat. "She means a lot to you, huh?"

"I want to make her happy."

"As long as she wants to make *you* happy too, you'll be set." Aidan clapped him on the shoulder. "After that last nightmare woman, you deserve a good one."

Hunter tossed Aidan his coat, and then sent Damon's jacket flying toward him. "We didn't think you'd ever be in a relationship again."

"What, were you taking bets on it?" The thought made him smile.

"No. But we were…" Pausing, Hunter frowned. "I guess concerned is the best word. You were in a dark place for a while."

He knew it. He also knew the way he felt about Emily far surpassed the way he'd ever felt about anyone. It was a little scary. "This thing with Emily is so much *more* than that mess with Ursula. You know? It's huge."

Aidan handed him the keys he'd left on the counter. "Then let's go find her that bracelet."

They headed out and took his SUV. The tight trio Damon had enjoyed with Hunter and Aidan would likely change even more once the weddings happened and the guys were living with their spouses, and even more than that if any of them had kids someday. The way he was thinking about Emily, he completely understood the guys wanting to be with their better halves, but even so, he missed his friends and intended to enjoy every second of their time together. "After this, dinner's on me. You guys can pick the place."

When they stood in the middle of the first store,

among all the pieces of jewelry from by-gone eras, he was sure the three of them looked as out of place as he felt.

An old man wearing an apron with the shop's logo came over to them. "May I help you find something?"

Damon nodded. "I'm looking for a women's gold ID bracelet. Nineteen-forties era. If one has the name Emily, that would be even better."

The man directed him to a glass case. "These are all that we have."

He looked through the names. No Emily. Disappointed, he stepped back.

"How about one of these?" The man held out four bracelets. "While names were the most common to place on the bracelets back then, we do have a few with endearments."

He lifted the first bracelet. Delicate links of gold, with *Darling* engraved on the plate. Darling. He rolled the word around in his head, but couldn't picture himself ever calling her *darling*. That just wasn't him. If he was going to get her something, he wanted it to feel right.

The next few weren't any better. He handed back the last one and shook his head. "Thanks for your time."

"Charm bracelets were popular back then as well." The clerk passed him another bracelet. Two tiny heart charms dangled from the silver links.

Damon turned it over, testing the links and the clasp. "This one could work."

It wasn't anywhere near a replacement for what

she'd lost, but it could be something that made her think of him whenever she wore it. "I'll take it."

He followed the clerk toward the register at the front of the shop. Beside the register, in a carved wooden box encased in glass, a small tray of rings gleamed.

One caught his attention, and he bent to study the shiny solitaire. Rather than one large stone, seven small diamonds were arranged in a cluster, the formation reminding him of a flower.

As he rose, the clerk was already reaching for the ring. "Would you like to see it?"

He nodded, afraid to look back at the guys and see their expressions. Would they think he was crazy?

"This is an illusion solitaire which showcases seven single cut natural diamonds. It's from the nineteen-forties." The clerk rambled on about the cut and quality as Damon stared at the ring.

The cluster of diamonds reminded him of something that had been broken and then pieced back together to be even better than the original. He turned the ring, and the heart woven into the band directly below the diamonds resembled an *E* turned on its side.

He could picture it on Emily's hand. Could picture himself sliding it in place. His heart throbbed at a faster pace as excitement laced through his body.

Wanting their support, he did look at the guys then. Both walked to him and flanked him on either side.

Hunter grinned. "When you know, you know."

Aidan nodded and smiled too. "When you picked this up, your face said it all. It's her ring."

He agreed. The ring warmed in his hand, and he didn't want to hand it back for even just the purchase. He nodded at them and then at the clerk. "I'll take it."

After they left the shop, he insisted they stop for a drink. They stopped at the nearest sports bar. Crowded into a small booth with beers and wings and nachos, he grinned as his buddies toasted him. Flying high on too much adrenaline, he kept touching his jacket pocket and feeling for the ring box.

Hunter picked up a chip loaded with salsa. "So when are you thinking of proposing?"

A sudden moment of worry that he was moving too fast—or that Emily would think he was moving too fast—flashed through him. "I don't know. I guess I don't have to rush it…"

"When the time's right, you'll know." Aidan tipped back his beer and then laughed. "Or the ring will burn a hole in your pocket until you're about to burst, like what happened to me. Go with whichever comes first."

Damon barely resisted the urge to check for the ring again. "The burning a hole in my pocket thing is already happening."

The noise level in the diner bordered on insane. Emily leaned over the table, straining to hear Kira and Skye's voices. After a long day of Christmas shopping, the last thing she needed was more noise and confusion, but the place was close to the stores and hunger had won out. "I missed that. What did you say?"

Skye's hair fell in a waterfall, covering the worst of her scars. In crowded settings, she seemed more at ease if Aidan was nearby, but he wasn't there, so Emily and Kira did their best to help. Playing with the ends of her scarf, she shifted closer. "I asked if everything was all set for the charity gala next week."

"Yep. Food, decorations, and the pro athletes' appearances are all confirmed. I'm glad I found a dress today. Otherwise, I don't know what I would have worn." The black and red gown had a low back and showed off her curves. She couldn't wait for Damon to see it.

"I loved that dress on you. You're going to look great."

"Thanks. I'm a little nervous about the event. I know the local news stations cover it every year, and this will be the first time I'll be face to face with some of my old associates since the whole thing happened with Paul. It might be awkward." She'd sworn she'd seen him driving in the area around Kallis Toys a handful of times over the last several days, but she couldn't be sure the man was, in fact, him. The driver had a different car than the one Paul had bought when they were together and the hat and sunglasses shielded his identity. She was glad she'd been honest about him to Damon. Forewarned was forearmed.

Kira placed a hand on her arm. "It'll be fine. And we'll all be right there with you if you need us."

Hearing that helped. Kira and Skye and the guys were a tight unit, and they'd all acted like she belonged. Having backup was a good feeling.

She wanted the party to be a success. After the difficult, stressful months the company had endured since the recall, everyone needed a fun and happy event to blow off some steam. The amount of money they'd raise for Children's Hospital would go a long way toward helping the kids there.

Kira motioned to the waitress for the check, then turned to them. "Did you need to go anywhere else?"

Emily drained the last of her coffee. "One last stop for me. I need to go to the sports collectibles store to pick up my dad's present."

Skye shook her head. "I'm shopped out. All I want to do is head home and crawl into bed. I hope we get back before Aidan gets home. I need to hide the presents."

Aidan, Hunter, and Damon were spending the day together. Emily hoped they were having a good time—not that they ever let anything get in their way. Damon had been looking forward to it, mentioning it more than once over the last week. She wanted him to be happy.

She also had no idea what to get him for Christmas. Nothing seemed quite right. With fourteen days to go, hopefully inspiration would strike soon.

Kira insisted on picking up the check, and then they loaded their bags and themselves into Skye's car, and Emily gave her directions to the sports store.

The bell chimed overhead when they walked in.

She waved at Steve behind the counter. He reached behind him and then set an envelope on the counter and withdrew the card she'd purchased.

"Thanks for finding this for me." She turned the card over, inspecting it. Near-mint condition, professionally graded a nine out of ten.

He smiled. "Happy to do it. I hope your dad likes it."

"He's going to be over the moon."

While Steve rang up her purchase, she perused the contents of the glass case, then did a double-take. There, resting on the top shelf, was a vintage Guy Proch rookie card.

Cards weren't serial numbered back when Proch played, so she had no way of knowing if it was the exact card that Damon had lost, but even if not, maybe having this one would help him feel better.

"Something else catch your interest?" Steve's voice pressed into her musings.

"Could I see the Guy Proch card?"

"That's a great one. Near-mint, like the one you just bought. I've only had it in for a few weeks."

Damon regretted selling that card, she'd seen it on his face and heard it in his voice. He'd been sad, frustrated, and angry when he'd spoken about it. And he'd seemed so pleased that she hadn't thought his hobby stupid.

Such a strong, caring man. Rebuilding all that had been stolen from him would take time, but maybe if he had this one card back, he'd regain part of what he'd lost. Maybe he'd fully regain his ability to trust.

"I'll take it."

Steve's brows rose. "Whoa. Your dad's one lucky guy."

"This one is for a friend." Friend? Boyfriend? Boss who she slept with? She and Damon hadn't put a label on their relationship, but she hoped that he considered her a friend at the very least.

The card cost triple the price of the one she'd bought for her dad, but she didn't care. It would make Damon happy.

She tucked the padded envelope with the cards into her purse, then joined Kira and Skye at the door.

Adjusting her scarf and gloves, Skye smiled. "Is that *friend* Damon?"

"Maybe." Then uncertainty washed through her pleasure. "Do you think it's too much? Do you think *he'll* think it's too much?"

Kira grinned and linked their arms together. "I think he'll be floored. And touched. And I wish I'd thought of it first."

A cold wind whipped around them as they walked to the car, but Emily didn't mind it as much as she had earlier. She mentally went through the wrapping paper she had at home. Which would be the best for his gift? The presentation was important to her. She liked the gifts to look perfect.

They hadn't discussed exchanging presents. She didn't know if he was planning on getting her anything or not. Holidays could be difficult and disappointing if expectations weren't met. And the pressure to do the "right" thing could be overwhelming. Damon's ex had sounded like a fairly demanding, high-maintenance person, so Emily hadn't brought up the topic of gifts at all. But maybe she should have. She didn't want him thinking that she expected the moon.

Hopefully, he knew that the only thing she really wanted was him.

CHAPTER THIRTEEN

The hotel ballroom glittered with white lights and sparkling Christmas ornaments. Holiday music pumped from the speakers, and wait staff dressed as elves in red and green costumes circulated the room with trays of holiday-themed hors d'oeuvres. The attendees had paid a good amount to mingle with the top stars from Buffalo's sports teams, and the athletes couldn't have been nicer or more accommodating.

Emily finished chatting with the community events reporter from Channel 5 and then directed her over to Damon and Kira's parents for a quote and some on-screen face time. The reporter was the second of the night. The Channel 8 reporter was hanging out with two of the Buffalo Bedlam players and a group of donors by the photo booth. Channel 10 hadn't sent anyone yet, and this late in the evening, there was a good chance no one would show.

A hand on her waist turned her, and all at once, she

was in Damon's arms. They'd been pulled in opposite directions the entire evening. He grinned down at her. Then he pulled away enough to twirl her in a circle. He groaned low and traced a finger over the deep V at her back. "I know I said this earlier, but damn, you look sexy."

"Thanks. You look good too." That was an understatement. In his tux, he looked incredible.

His hand continued to trace patterns on her skin, sending tingles down her spine. "You did a great job with this party."

"I hope everyone is having a good time. I really want it to be successful." Most of the Kallis Toys employees were there. She wanted to impress them, and she wanted to make Damon proud. She knew he thought that she was a good assistant, but this was the first public party that she'd helped plan, and everyone knew that she'd managed it.

He didn't look worried at all. "The thing people remember most is the food, and I've been hearing nothing but praise for the chefs."

She'd take his word for it. Her stomach had been too nervous to accept anything more than a few sips of water.

"Dance with me." He extended his hand.

"But, I should check on—"

"The dance floor. I agree." His eyes lit with his smile. "Come on. Please?"

She couldn't resist. They joined the other few couples, and she slid her arms around Damon's neck, breathing him in and holding him close. "People are staring. This is going to cause some gossip about you and me."

His hands were warm on her back, and his fingers gently kneaded her muscles. He bent his head until his lips hovered by her ear. "I don't care. Let them talk. I've wanted to do this all night. And later, maybe you'll come home with me."

She shivered as his breath tickled her skin. "We won't have to wait much longer before the night's over."

His parents were due to present the check to the director of Children's Hospital soon, and the gala was scheduled to end in an hour. Then she could go home and slip off her heels and into her cozy snowflake pajamas. But for now, she'd put the worrying over the party on hold and relish these minutes with having Damon all to herself. They swayed together, bodies brushing and teasing her oversensitive nerves.

After a few more songs, they wandered away from the dance floor and met some of the athletes, and then moved to hang out with Hunter and Kira and Aidan and Skye by the dessert table. All the while, Emily kept checking on food and drinks, making sure the tables stayed full, but the wait staff was efficient, and she didn't have to do any prompting.

As the minutes ticked closer toward the party's end, she relaxed more and more, feeling like the evening had been a success.

Damon snagged two glasses of champagne from a

passing waiter and handed one to her. "You should be proud. You pulled off a great event."

"I'm happy." The past week had been busy, but all of her triple-checking had paid off. "I didn't see Caleb. Wasn't he coming?"

"I saw him this afternoon. He told me he'd have to skip tonight. I think he wanted to be with Gwen."

"We should stop in and visit her next week."

"I like that you care so much."

She sipped her champagne. "Gwen's a sweet kid."

"You're pretty sweet yourself." He set their glasses aside, and then bent and kissed her.

"Excuse me." The familiar voice sent shockwaves through Emily. Paul stood before them, with a Channel 10 camera rolling.

She did a double-take. What the hell was *he* doing there? The news stations sent the community events reporters to cover the events like galas, or on occasion, they'd send a meteorologist for them to do a live weather report on-site, but never an investigative reporter. She didn't like the sinister smirk on Paul's face. Not one bit. Her stomach clenched, but she stared him down.

His eyes flicked to meet Emily's gaze, then he directed his focus toward Damon. "Mr. Kallis, if I may have a word?"

Damon's body tightened, but he pulled away from Emily and nodded. "We're happy to be able to donate a large sum to Children's Hospital tonight, and we thank our attendees and athletes for making that happen."

"No. Not about that." Paul's eyes gleamed with the triumphant glee of a hot story. He held out his phone. An image of the teddy bear prototype covered the screen, followed by a picture of the design plans. "The new prototype of the teddy bear you're working on is a walking, talking model. Can you tell our viewers at home what steps you're taking to guarantee the next generation of the toys won't explode, considering the larger battery size you'll need? And what about the design flaw that makes them likely to tip over? And is it true that you're rushing the testing to put this product on the market in time for Valentine's Day?"

Damon's thunderous expression promised violence. "Where the hell did you get that information?"

Paul thrust his microphone in Damon's face. "Child safety is at stake. Don't you think the public deserves to know?"

Anger burned through Damon's muscles. He whipped his gaze from the phone to the asshole reporter's face. "I repeat: where the hell did you get your information?"

"A reporter never reveals his sources, and I can be very resourceful." A smirk accompanied Paul's words.

Damon forced down the urge to grab the guy and shake or punch the answer out of him. No one outside the company had that information. Which meant he had a mole, and he didn't like that one bit. "You can tell your source and everyone else that there's no way we'd release the toy until we're one hundred percent positive about its safety."

"Really? Even with the amount of money your company lost with the recall?"

Ready to snap off the guy's head, he advanced a step with his hands clenched into fists. "No one questions our integrity—"

Two hands clamped on his shoulders from behind and yanked him back. And then his father stepped in front of him and faced down the reporter. "In the forty years that I've been involved with the toy industry, I've never compromised on safety. If you have any other questions, please forward them to me through our PR Department. This is a party and my employees, guests, and donors deserve to celebrate. I'll have to ask you to leave."

Three members of hotel security came forward and the large and imposing men began to escort the reporter and cameraman toward the ballroom's exit. As the roaring in Damon's ears faded, the absence of conversations in the large room captured his attention. Everywhere he looked, all eyes were on him, his father, and Paul.

Paul half-turned as he was led away. His gaze shot to Emily and then he winked at her. "That's fine. I still have my source."

Damon stood rooted to his spot as several of his employees stared at him and then at each other.

Who the hell had shared the photo and the plans?

The toy company never had something like this

happen before. They treated their employees like family. Everyone knew the prototype's importance.

The background of the photo had definitely been the design room. He began counting off the present employees. Several members of the design team were grouped together by the food tables. Would one of them have been stupid enough to leak the information? Or, had another of his employees gone in and taken the photo?

The champagne and hors d'oeuvres bunched in his gut at the ugly realization that someone in their extended toy family had betrayed their trust.

His dad grabbed a microphone and told everyone to go back to enjoying the party. Conversations quickly resumed, and Damon had no doubt that the altercation with Paul was the topic.

Feeling rooted to his spot, he cast a glance around the room for Aidan and Hunter. He needed to meet with them and his parents and sister to develop a plan. There was no time to waste in starting the investigation into who leaked the information.

Emily moved to his side. "I'm so sorry. Paul is a massive jerk. Are you okay?"

He stared at her with fresh eyes as his thoughts spiraled. Paul had winked at her when he'd said that line about still having his source. He'd been her ex, and she'd been an investigative reporter for years. Had she lied about her situation with Paul? Had she really been looking for a job, or had that been a ruse to get the scoop on the toy? Had she used her friendship with Kira? Used him?

"We've had the same employees in R&D, in most of our departments, for years. Nothing like this has ever happened before." The only new addition was Emily. Maybe a coincidence. Maybe not.

He couldn't believe she could be involved. Would she go so far as to feign interest in him to gain his confidence and steal company secrets? The thought made him sick—but he'd been used by an unscrupulous girlfriend before...

But how would Emily have taken a photo of prototype without his knowledge? Then, in a flash, he remembered that she'd taken a walk down to R&D a few days earlier to drop off present for Caleb to give to Gwen. And, she'd had access to the prototype plans when she organized the files. So she had a possible motive, and she definitely had the opportunity.

His stomach hurt like he'd taken a direct hit to his solar plexus. He'd actually been thinking that she was the woman for him. He'd bought that damn ring. For someone who might have used him for personal gain. Had he made a colossal error in judgment again? His head ached, and his heart ripped open.

But this betrayal didn't just hurt him. This affected every single person in his company. People he considered friends and family.

"Our competitors now know what we were planning," his voice rasped the awful reality, "and they have the picture and enough information to help them. If they beat us to the punch, we will have to do that layoff after all."

"I'm so sorry." She squeezed his hand. "How can we fix it?"

He extracted his hand from her grip and stepped away. He couldn't let her touch him, not when he wasn't sure. "I need to be able to trust my people. My first step is finding the leak before any more information is made public."

Her forehead wrinkled, and she stared at the space he'd created between them. "You know I used to be a reporter. I'm good at digging into things. I can help."

"I can't let you help."

Her eyes widened, and her mouth opened then closed as she realized his insinuation. "Because I'm under investigation too? I didn't do it, Damon, if that's what you're implying. I wouldn't hurt you or your family that way."

He wanted to believe her innocence. But he couldn't. Not yet. He couldn't fire her or anyone else. Not until he had proof. But he could take steps to distance himself.

"I need to move you out of my office." It would become his fortress once more. He was better off that way.

"I see." She bit her lip. "There aren't any open cubicles on the floor."

He sighed and rubbed his hands over his face. "Hunter will figure it out."

"Maybe it's just better for me to give my notice. You want to get rid of me. That seems to be the easiest way."

He lowered his hands. The thought that she was

leaving because "the job" was finished flashed through his mind.

She drew herself up, shoulders back and head held high. "I won't work for a company that doesn't believe in me. Not ever again. You'll have a formal resignation notice on your desk Monday morning."

Before he could say anything more, she walked away, and he was left standing there, pissed off and hurt, and unable to figure out who to believe or what to do.

CHAPTER FOURTEEN

On Monday morning, Emily bypassed the break room and went straight to Damon's office. Gossip from passing employees filtered into her thoughts. Everyone was speculating about who had leaked the information and what was going to happen to the employee if they were found out.

She'd spent the weekend at her parents' house, helping to get their house ready for hosting Christmas Eve dinner, and had kept her phone turned off the entire time. The busywork had kept her hands occupied, and she'd managed to brush off questions about Damon and her job without showing the hurt and anger she'd been jumping back and forth between since Friday evening.

After leaving the party, she'd run into Kira. Everyone had been reeling from the news, but from Kira's reaction, she knew her friend hadn't questioned her innocence one bit.

Too bad she couldn't say the same for Damon.

That hurt cut deep. Deeper than she'd known she could hurt.

Relationships were built on trust. If they didn't have that, they didn't have anything.

His office door was closed. She knocked, and then used her key for the last time. The soft jingle of the bells when she pushed the door open was enough to cause a lump in her throat.

He sat huddled around his desk with Aidan and Hunter, and all three heads turned in her direction. From their open laptops and papers covered in notes, the investigation was already underway.

Clutching her purse strap, she walked into the room. "Don't worry, this won't take long."

Damon's gaze locked on hers. He looked exhausted. "Guys, give us a minute."

His friends slowly rose, and both laid a hand on his shoulder, standing like sentries on either side of him. A united front, the guys were extremely protective of each other.

She forced herself to meet their gazes when they approached, curious as to whether they'd give away their feelings. Did they think she was guilty too? Aidan's eyes were unreadable, but he nodded at her, and Hunter's features were stoic, but he touched her shoulder as he passed. She had no doubt they'd wait right outside the door in case Damon needed them.

Nerves needling her stomach and an ache welling in

her chest, she pulled her resignation letter from her purse and laid it on his cluttered blotter. "I gave you the standard two weeks' notice, but my leaving today is probably better."

He stared at the paper but didn't touch it. "You don't have to go."

"If you can't trust me, then how can I stay?" She sighed and glanced around his office—formerly their office—memorizing the way everything looked.

His phone rang. He punched a button and silenced the call.

She needed to leave. Standing around and prolonging her exit wouldn't help anything. Boxing up her few belongings wasn't worth the effort, not when she'd be reminded of him every time she saw them.

The key clicked against his desk when she set it down. Remembering how he'd looked when he'd handed it over the first time wasn't going to help either.

Only one thing remained unfinished. She dug into her purse and extracted the small square box wrapped in shiny red paper, and set it on top of her resignation. "I found this for you a few weeks ago. Even after all that's happened, not giving it to you seemed silly. So anyway…" She backed away. "I'll let you get back to work."

He stood, sighing. "Emily, wait."

His phone rang again, and he swore. Then Aidan poked his head into the room. "Sorry to interrupt. One of your team members said your ten o'clock appointment is here."

Emily kept moving. The pressure in her chest was unbearable. "You're a busy man. And I need to go."

She closed the door behind her. The soft jingle of bells would forever be cemented in her mind with the end of her relationship with Damon.

On Christmas Eve morning, Damon sat at his desk, staring at the present Emily had given him five days earlier. The work week had passed in a whirlwind of meetings with the board, and lawyers, and interviewing employee after employee after employee.

Morale was at an all-time low. Gossip was running rampant. Speculations were being cast around. That afternoon's employee Christmas party was on course to be a dismal failure.

He'd tucked the gift into his desk after she'd left, unable to handle it then because the shock and hurt had still been so overwhelming and raw.

As the shock faded, the ache in his heart had only grown stronger. He missed her. He wanted her back.

It had taken him a few days to figure out that he'd never really believed that she would betray him. She knew what it was like to be used. He couldn't think of anyone less inclined to hurt another person.

What an impulsive fool he'd been.

But she wasn't answering her phone and the times he'd driven to her house, she hadn't been home. He wasn't sure what to do.

He carefully tore the wrapping paper and lifted the lid. Through the tissue paper, he glimpsed the Bedlam's old logo on a printed surface.

What the—

A card. It had to be a card. He pushed the paper aside. Neatly framed in the bottom of the box lay Guy Proch's rookie card. His throat tightened around the lump pounding at its base.

The card was graded higher than the one he'd had.

That she'd think enough of him to buy this...

Eyes tingling, he set the gift aside and walked to her desk. The snowman coffee cup, the candy cane striped pen, the sparkly snowflake sticker on her laptop. The matching Christmas trees on both their desks. The damn jingle bells on the doorknob. She'd brought light and color and happiness to his fortress. To his life.

And he'd ruined it all.

He had to get her back.

The ringing of his phone drew him to his desk. He snatched it up, impatient with the interruption. "Damon Kallis."

"Mr. Kallis, this is Andrea, I'm a nurse at Children's Hospital. One of our patient's parents turned in the bracelet you reported missing. They found it in the bottom of the gift bag your company gave their son when you were all here for your holiday visit."

No way.

Talk about a freaking Christmas miracle. That gift bag could have ended up in the trash, and the bracelet lost forever.

Energy charged his system. "Thanks. I'll head over now."

"I'm on the fifth floor. Just ask for me at the nurse's station."

He grabbed his coat and rushed out of the office, stopping long enough to lock his door and tell his team he'd be gone for a while. He'd have at least one more chance with Emily when he returned the bracelet.

The drive to the hospital was easy and familiar, but the scent of the place still stung his nose—antiseptic and something else he couldn't name. He met with the nurse and recovered the bracelet. A broken clasp was the reason it had fallen off Emily's wrist. He tucked the bracelet safely in his pocket and then gave the nurse a bag filled with toys for the kid who'd found it.

When he turned to leave, he spotted Caleb sitting in Gwen's room with his face buried in his hands, shoulders shaking like he was crying.

Had Caleb received bad news about Gwen? A worse diagnosis? Stomach tightening, he crossed the hallway, and his concern grew when he saw Gwen's empty bed. He sat beside him and patted the man's shoulder. "Caleb? Are you okay?"

Caleb looked at him and cringed. "I screwed up. Big time. I'm an awful person."

Shit. He wished Aidan were there. Aidan knew how to handle emotions a lot better. "What's going on?"

"I… I made a mistake, and it's going to hurt the company."

Damon exhaled and relaxed. Gwen was okay. "If it's another setback with the prototype, don't worry about it until after the new year. Enjoy the week off with your family."

"No. It's…" He sighed and then stood, his expression a combination of sadness and fear. "I'm the one who leaked the info to Paul Redmond."

Damon staggered back, his muscles rigid under now icy skin and anger boiling in his blood. "What? Why?"

"I needed money. Gwen's hospital bills are piling up. Paul caught me driving out of the employee parking lot a few weeks ago and followed me home. He said he'd pay me for information about the toy, so I gave him what he wanted. But I've felt so guilty, I haven't used the money yet."

"Why the hell wouldn't you have come to me?" Slamming his fist into the door, he gritted out the words. "You've worked for us for over ten years. You know how we are. How my parents treat everyone like family. If you needed help taking care of Gwen, you should have just asked. Hell, I've *offered* to help you. What do you think I meant all the times I've said *let me know if you need anything*?"

"I figured you meant more time off. How could I come to you and ask for help paying her bills?"

He was pissed. His muscles burned with the desire to punch something instead of the door. "I was waiting until the Christmas party to share this with you, but the company had decided to cover all of the costs of Gwen's treatment that aren't covered by insurance."

Caleb's mouth gaped open. "You... You were going to do all that for me?"

"We've set up a fund for her. My parents didn't want you worrying about anything other than spending time with your little girl."

"I can't believe it." His voice cracked, and he pressed his fist to his forehead as he fought for control. "I'm so sorry. I got scared and wasn't thinking clearly."

"Do you know what I've lost because of this?" Damon wanted to throttle him. Disappointment settled heavily in the pit of his stomach.

"I'm sorry. I know the team will have to put in extra hours to make sure no one beats us to the punch with releasing the toy. And that means paying them overtime."

That wasn't what he meant. At the moment, he couldn't care less about the damn prototype or overtime pay.

A nurse wheeled Gwen into the room. Clutching her stuffed white cat in one hand, the child waved. "Daddy, I didn't cry this time."

Fresh tears rolled down Caleb's face. Sniffling, he brushed them away. "I'm proud of you, sweetheart. But if you had cried, that's okay too."

She grinned at Damon. "Mr. Damon, did Miss Emily come with you?"

He tamped down his anger and found a smile for her. "Today, it's just me."

Caleb stepped toward her and ruffled her cat's fur. "Sweetheart, I'll be right back. I need to talk to Mr. Damon in the hall."

Damon led him to an alcove that would give them the most privacy. His mind flashed through everything that had happened. Never in a million years would he have suspected Caleb.

His lead engineer regarded him with sorrow in his gaze. "I can't apologize enough. Your family has been nothing but good to me, and I screwed up royally. I have a few personal things on my desk, a picture of Gwen and some drawings she made me. Can you have them sent to me please?"

Damon couldn't bear what he was hearing and closed his eyes to concentrate. Anger, betrayal, pity, and understanding swirled like a tornado. He could barely wrap his head around Caleb's confession. The man had worked for his company for the past ten years.

True, he'd made a deliberate deal. A huge error in judgment. All out of desperation to save his child. What would his own father have done to save him or Kira? Or any father, in any life or death situation? "Look, Caleb. I'm not going to make any rash decisions right now."

"You're not going to fire me?"

"I need to talk to my family first." It wasn't his call anyway. His parents had to make that decision.

"If it helps, I'll return the money."

"Doing that won't make the leaked information

disappear. He gave it to you. Use it or donate it to the hospital. And as far as Gwen's medical expenses, we'll still work something out."

"You'd help me even after this?"

Gwen didn't deserve to suffer because of her father's mistake. "Again, I need to talk to my family. But yeah."

Caleb stared at the floor. "Whether or not you fire me, I need to apologize to your parents, my co-workers, and everyone else. I think some of the guys in R&D suspected it was me. The guilt has been awful. Can I make an announcement at the employee party this afternoon? I don't want anyone else suffering through the holidays because they're worried about a possible mole in their department or that they're going to get fired by mistake."

"I'm not sure if that's a good idea." In fact, he thought it wouldn't be a wise idea at all. "Let me think about it a bit."

"That's fair. You'll call me?"

"Yeah. Keep your phone on. I have to go."

As soon as he reached the parking garage, he called his parents and told them about Caleb's confession. Of course, they wanted to speak to the man, and as soon as possible. He called Caleb and told him to head into the office to meet with his parents before to the Christmas party at three o'clock.

Then he called Emily. It went straight to voicemail, just like it had all week.

He drove to her house, but her car wasn't in the driveway.

Sitting there, he dialed again. Again, voicemail. This time, he left a message. "Emily, it's Damon. Call me. Please. It's important."

Then he called his sister, filled her in about Caleb, and asked for help in tracking down Emily.

Kira was still ticked off at him for how he'd reacted, but at least she was talking to him again. "Emily is at her parents' house, helping to get things ready for their dinner tonight. You better fix this, Damon, or I'll—"

"I get it. Do you think you can convince her to come to the employee party this afternoon? Dad's going to make some type of announcement about Caleb. When it's my turn to speak, I thought I'd try to fix things with Emily."

"I honestly don't know if she'd come. I wouldn't if I were her. It might be better to have Aidan call and say he needs her to sign something for HR, and he needs it taken care of today."

It was worth a try, but if it didn't work, he was going to camp out on her doorstep until he could convince her to talk to him.

A few hours later, with the heavily decorated party well underway, he stood with Aidan and Hunter, waiting for his dad to give his speech, and staring at the door willing Emily to arrive.

Time had passed in a blink. After Caleb had spoken

to his parents, Damon and Kira sat down with them. He'd only seen his parents get that angry and upset on a handful of occasions. The Toy Factory was their dream, their life, and no one had expected that one of their employees would ever undermine their trust.

Other than Kira, the only ones who knew the truth about Caleb were Aidan and Hunter.

Aidan grabbed a cookie off a tray. "You've been staring at the door for fifteen minutes. She said she'd try to stop by, but let me remind you that she didn't sound enthusiastic. And I hate lying, so now I have to come up with a form for her to sign if she does show up."

His parents walked to the front of the room, and his dad waited until conversations died down. "First, I want to thank you all for how hard you've worked this year. The company made some great strides and had a few setbacks, but I'm proud to have each of you as part of the Kallis Toys family."

Damon turned his head. In the corner of his vision, Emily came into view. She stood with Kira by the entrance. Moving in the middle of the speeches would be a distraction. He'd need to wait until they were finished.

His mom nodded. "We'd like to address the incident that's been on everyone's minds. The employee who leaked the information has come forward and has been placed on administrative leave while we work through everything. The company will come through this stronger than ever, and we thank you all for your loyalty and commitment."

Murmurs and whispers started up all around him as people tried to figure out which employees were missing from the party. Caleb wasn't in attendance, and only a small handful of employees weren't there.

Damon strode to his parents, ready to make his speech. But when he turned to face the crowd, he didn't see Emily standing among the sea of faces. He finally made eye contact with Kira, and his sister shook her head and pointed to the door.

Emily was gone.

His stomach sank and frustration surged. He gave a quick speech thanking his team and all of the employees for their hard work over the year, and then turned the floor over to his dad again. Scanning the room for Emily on the off chance that she'd returned, he missed whatever his dad said, but everyone applauded. And then the crowd dispersed and people surrounded him, asking questions, wishing him a happy holiday, chatting about the party and their plans for the coming year. Damon fought against the urge to rush from the room and gave the employees his attention.

Moving through the conversations as quickly as he could still took the better part of an hour. Finally, he made his way to Kira. "Where is she?"

"She went to her parents' house."

He turned to leave, then realized he didn't know where he was going. "Text me the address."

She crossed her arms and narrowed her eyes. "You better make it clear that she has her job back."

"I will. I know how bad I screwed up. The most important thing is making sure she'll take me back."

Her eyes softened, and she hugged him tight. "They aren't too far from here. You'd better go. I'll text the address right now."

"Thanks." He rushed to his car.

Twenty minutes later, he pulled up beside the crowded driveway of the large home. Lights twinkled from every window. He grabbed her present off the seat and took a deep breath.

He wasn't sure what she'd told her family, or how hard he'd have to fight to get inside, but he wasn't leaving without talking to her. Determination firing through his muscles, he strode up the snow-lined path and rang the bell.

Moments later, the door swung open. Emily stood before him in a white dress, with her hair streaming around her shoulders, and hurt deep in her gaze. She crossed her arms over her chest. "What are you doing here?"

Light shone off her hair shone like a halo. In her white dress, she was his very own Christmas angel. He swallowed hard against his suddenly thick throat. "Apologizing and begging you to come back to me."

She pulled the door closed at her back and stood with him on the steps. "Damon, this isn't—"

"Look," he cut her off before she had a chance to shut him down. "I was an idiot. Deep down, I knew you wouldn't hurt my family or me that way. And I realized that before I found out who leaked the information.

Instead of thinking rationally, I jumped back to what had happened to me before. That was wrong."

"Your reaction cut me to the core. I know your ex used you, and that's a hard thing to get over. But you can't assume I'm the same as she is."

"I know. And I'm sorry." Shifting the box to the crook of his arm, he grasped her hands. "Please don't let my stupidity end what we have."

"I'm afraid you're not over what your ex did to you."

"I've had time to think about that. You're nothing like her. You're helping me heal." He thought again about those Christmas decorations. "You brought light and happiness back to me. Back to my heart. I need you in my life."

She hesitated, but her expression softened the tiniest bit. "It's not easy to erase the hurt I felt."

"Whatever you want me to do, I'll do it. Let me prove it to you." Desperate to convince her how much she meant to him, he tightened his grasp on her hands and his voice took on the urgency coursing through his body. "I love you, Emily. Won't you let me show you?"

Her brows rose, highlighting the vulnerability in her gaze. A sigh escaped her full lips before she spoke. "I want to say yes."

Relief began to sprout. Damon stepped back and pulled her resignation letter from his pocket and then tore it into small pieces. "I'm not accepting this. Work isn't the same without you. Nothing is."

Her eyes sparkled with tears and her voice cracked

as she spoke, "You make it really hard for me to stay angry."

"Does this mean I'm forgiven?"

She nodded and her hands gripped his once again. Holding on tight. Binding them together. "But you need to talk to me instead of shutting down and shutting me out."

"From now on. I promise." The ache in his heart had disappeared. In its place, contentment and joy bloomed. He leaned in and kissed her, and the warmth in his chest spread to his whole body.

The box dug into his arm. He pulled back and held it out to her. "This is for you."

"Should I wait to open it?"

"Open it now." He couldn't wait to see her expression. "I opened my present today. And I need to thank you. I can't believe you got me that card. I know it wasn't cheap. It means more to me than anything I've ever received."

Her smile rivaled the gleaming lights framing the door. "I wanted to make you happy and to help you get back something you'd lost. I'd do anything for you."

Delicate fingers pulled at the ribbon, and then she lifted the lid off the box. Her eyes rounded, and she gasped. "My bracelet! How did you find it?"

She pulled the bracelet free, turning it over and over in her hands.

"It was in one of the gift bags for the hospital kids. The clasp is broken. It must have fallen off when we were putting the bags into my car or carrying them into the hospital. I got a phone call this morning, and when I went to the hospital to pick it up, Caleb was there visiting with Gwen. That's when he broke down and admitted leaking the info to Paul, who it turns out, offered a lot of money for the info. With Gwen's expenses piling up, Caleb caved in."

"How awful. I'm so sorry for him and for you."

"Not as sorry as I am. I almost lost you."

"What's going to happen to Caleb?"

"He's on paid leave for the next few weeks until we sort this out and figure out what to do. Something like this has never happened before. He'll probably end up keeping his job, but I'm not sure if it'll be the same one. He's a good man, he just made a really bad choice. We're still going to set up that fund for Gwen."

"That's generous of the company. But what about the prototype?"

He shrugged. "We'll get it out when it's ready. Kira has some marketing ideas about letting the consumers vote for some more modifications we're thinking of making, so they'll feel like they had a hand in building it. Hopefully, that will help sales and keep customers loyal to us if a competitor tries to release it first."

"It sounds like things will work out well for you."

"The only way things are working out well is if I have you."

She trailed her fingers along his jaw. "You do."

At those words, his eyes closed and he reveled in the feeling of belonging, of acceptance, of love. He pointed to the box. "There's one more thing in there, under the first layer of tissue paper."

She dug through and found the second bracelet and held it up to the light. "This is beautiful."

"It's from the same time period. I thought the two hearts linked together was a good representation of us."

Her gaze lifted to his, soft and shimmery. "I agree. Help me put it on?"

His fingers felt clumsy handling such a small clasp, but he managed. The charms jingled when she dropped her hand, and he thought of the jingle bells in his office. "I called the place where I purchased the bracelet and asked if they also do repairs. They do, but they weren't able to fit it in today. We can drop it off on the twenty-sixth, and they said you might even have it back the same day."

Emily cupped one hand on the back of his neck and drew him toward her. She kissed him and he lost himself in the feeling of having her in his arms again and the way the meeting of lips charged through him like electricity. After a long moment, she pulled him toward the house. "Can you stay? Meet my family? Have dinner with us?"

"I was hoping that invitation was still open."

He followed her inside. Music and laughter flowed from the dining room and kitchen. Damon stopped in front of the huge tree dripping with lights and ornaments in the living room. "Hold on for just a second."

She turned to him and slipped her arms around his waist. "Yes?"

He framed her face with his hands. "Thank you for giving me another chance."

"I love you, Damon. And I need you too." Smiling, she leaned into him and pressed a soft kiss to his lips.

Happiness as bright as a Christmas star filled his soul. "That's the best present I could have received."

Sharing his smile, she eased back and then linked their fingers together. "Come meet my family. They're going to love you as much as I do."

CHAPTER FIFTEEN

Dodging Christmas snow flurries, Damon grasped Emily's hand and rushed to Kira's front door. They were late. Really late. The twelve text messages he'd received were evidence enough. But he hadn't been able to help himself. He'd been too busy enjoying being with Emily on a cozy Christmas morning to pay attention to simple things like the time, or that they were supposed to have arrived at his sister's house over an hour ago.

Hunter opened the door and waved them inside. "We were about to send out a search party."

"Smart ass." He hugged him and then greeted his sister, his parents, and Aidan and Skye.

Emily shrugged out of her coat. "I'm sorry we're late. We lost track of time."

"I'll bet." Aidan murmured behind Damon. Turning, Damon elbowed his friend in the stomach and then stole his beer.

Aidan just grinned and grabbed another bottle from the table. "You look happy."

"I am happy."

Actually, he was ecstatic.

After spending Christmas Eve with Emily's family, and chatting about collectibles and cards with her dad, he'd gone home with her and had spent hours showing her how grateful he was that she'd given them a second chance. Then he'd woken up with the best gift, having Emily next to him. They'd shared a lazy morning of snuggling followed by coffee and cinnamon rolls in front of the twinkling Christmas tree.

Hunter joined them. "Are you going to do it?"

Damon glanced over his shoulder, making sure Emily was out of earshot. She stood on the opposite side of the room, engrossed in a conversation with Kira and Skye. He turned back to his friends and closed his hand around the tiny box in his pocket. When he and Emily had stopped by his place so he could grab a change of clothes, he'd snagged the ring. "I'm ready."

"I'll call everyone into the kitchen to give you some privacy." Hunter patted him on the shoulder. "I'm happy for you."

"She still has to say yes."

Aidan pulled the beer from Damon's hand. "Somehow, I don't see her saying no. I'll just hold this for you."

Damon walked over to Emily and wrapped his arms around her. She leaned into him as she continued her conversation.

"Everyone, come into the kitchen." Hunter beckoned them to the other room. "We're going to make a Christmas toast and you'll all need a glass of champagne."

The group moved toward the kitchen, and Damon stayed in his spot, holding Emily in his arms. Laughing, she twisted to face him. "We're already bad guests for showing up so late. We should go in so they aren't waiting for us even more."

"In a minute. There's something I want to do first." Grasping her hand, he led her to the bay window overlooking the front yard. Standing there, they were partially hidden behind the Christmas tree. Soft music piped from the speakers in the wall, filling the air with carols and sleigh bells. "I know we already exchanged gifts, but I have one more for you."

"You do?"

He pulled out the ring. The illusion solitaire caught the glittering lights on the tree. "I know we haven't been together that long, but my heart recognized you right away. Every day with you has been a gift. I want a life-time more. Will you marry me?"

She raised her hands to her heart and her gaze lifted to his. "Damon."

The breathlessness of her voice and the smile on her lips prompted him to remove the ring from the box. Her hand reached toward him, and he slid the ring home.

They'd come together when they were both jaded and tired, but their relationship had breathed new life into them. The bond they shared was formed by love and understanding and commitment and caring.

"I love you." Her arms encircled his neck, and her lips closed over his in a deep kiss.

He gave into the thrilling and comforting sensation of holding her close. "I love you too."

A throat cleared behind them. He raised his head. Hunter and Aidan stood side by side, grinning. Behind them, Kira and Skye and his parents gathered around.

"So," he said, as he stepped back and took Emily's hand. "We're engaged."

The room erupted in cheers. Kira pushed in first and hugged them both. "I hoped it would work out this way."

He exchanged hugs with his parents, then Skye, and then hugs with Hunter and Aidan while Kira and Skye and his mom admired Emily's ring.

His mom hugged Emily. "I'm happy Damon found such a wonderful woman."

Clapping Damon on the back, his dad looked far too pleased. "Now aren't you glad I forced you to hire an assistant?"

"Yep. This is all thanks to you." And to Kira, for bringing Emily into his life. Damon smiled, feeling at peace. All he wanted was right there in the room with him.

When the group began to scatter, lured by the food and drinks, he clasped Emily's hand in his and brought it to his lips.

He knew he'd never regret the day he asked her to be his wife. "Welcome to the family."

Her gaze lifted from their joined hands to his eyes. "Am I all you'll ever want for Christmas?"

"All I ever want, at Christmas, at any time of year, is you." And then he held her close as the tree lights twinkled and sleigh bells jingled, and his heart filled with love for his Christmas wish come true.

Thank you so much for reading *All I Want*! I would appreciate it if you would help others enjoy this book too! Please recommend to others and leave a review.

Don't miss the other books in the Holiday Hearts NY series:

Kiss Me Again

Kira Kallis is newly thirty, tired of being single, and wants to find someone special in time for Valentine's Day. After spending years focusing on her career, she has a great job, and supportive family and friends, but life as the perpetual third wheel is lonely. Creating an online dating profile was the easy part. Navigating the lines between truth and illusion in her "matches" is a lot harder.

Hunter York has been friends with Kira for years. From morning runs to chats over coffee at the office, he loves the time they spend together. But it can't go further than that. She's his best friend's sister, his co-worker, and off-limits for too many reasons. When he learns that she's using a dating site, he insists on checking into her matches who draw too many questions and yield not nearly enough answers. Overprotective or not, he cares too much to risk anything happening to her.

The more time they spend together, the harder it is to deny their connection and chemistry. Kira begins to wonder if the perfect match could have been by her side all along, and Hunter struggles with what could happen if he discards all the reasons he's wrong for her. But taking that step means going beyond paper hearts and chocolate-flavored kisses. It could mean risking a friendship they've both grown to depend on.

More Than Words

Aidan MacKay may be cool, calm, and collected in his Human Resources position for his Army buddy's toy company, but his battle with PTSD is anything but easy. Things change when he hires voiceover artist Skye Galen to record several company projects. Her voice calm, soothing, and just what Aidan needs. Their exchanges through email and phone calls only make him want more.

Skye has her own demons. After being burned in a fire, she's become a near-recluse. Hiding from the world is easier than facing people's reactions. She is intrigued by Aidan and yearns for more but doesn't believe he can see past her scars.

Aidan is determined to meet the woman behind the voice. Skye knows she'll have to brave the meeting if she wants her lucrative contract with his company to continue.

Sparks fly, and they begin a tentative relationship. But Aidan fears his PTSD may scare Skye away. And Skye worries her insecurities will eventually push Aidan away.

As the fourth of July draws near, fireworks are a guarantee, but they'll both have to face their biggest fears if they don't want their love to implode.

Marry Me

Join Kira and Hunter from Kiss Me Again, Aidan and Skye from More Than Words, and Emily and Damon from All I Want as they say their I do's.

Kira and Hunter have been planning their wedding for months. When their venue goes up in smoke two months before their big day, they are left scrambling to find a new location.

Engaged for four months, Skye and Aidan have held

off on making wedding plans. Aidan fears that Skye is getting cold feet, but Skye's reluctance stems from her mother's overbearing behavior. Still, she can't put off the wedding forever. She just wants a way to celebrate without the focus being so much on herself.

And newly-engaged Damon can't wait to marry Emily, but her family is insisting on a wedding venue that's booked solid for the next three years. He's not happy about waiting but doesn't see a way around it. Emily longs for something more unique and personal but is afraid to hurt the family by breaking with tradition.

When Emily recommends her favorite vacation spot as a substitute venue for Kira and Hunter, moving the wedding from Holiday, NY to Virginia Beach, VA, Damon sees an opportunity to solve all three couples' problems—a triple wedding.

But a March nor'easter bearing down on the East Coast the weekend of their wedding spells disaster for the couples. And that's only the beginning.

Find all of the Holiday Hearts stories:
https://www.susanscottshelley.com/holidayhearts

ABOUT THE AUTHOR

USA TODAY bestselling author Susan Scott Shelley writes romance with heat and heart that celebrates love without limits. She enjoys watching hockey, training for her next run, reading romance novels, and binging episodes of her favorite British TV shows. Susan lives in Philadelphia with her husband and also works as a professional voice over artist. A city girl who likes being out in nature as often as possible, she has yet to meet a plant she hasn't wanted to take home and she really wants a pet crow.

Visit her website: https://susanscottshelley.com

ALSO BY SUSAN SCOTT SHELLEY

Philadelphia Power series

Against the Rush, Over the Top, Behind the Mask, From the First, Powered by Love (series collection)

Love & Rugby series

Spiral, Spark, Smolder, Shine, Surprise, Swoon,

Love & Rugby vol.1, Love & Rugby, vol.2, Love & Rugby, the complete collection

Love & Rugby: Season of Love series

Savor, Seduce, Stay,

Love & Rugby: Season of Love, the complete collection

Pride of the Bedlam series

Skating On Chance, Holding On Tight, Scoring Slater, Playing with Pride (series collection)

Buffalo Bedlam Series

Making His Move, Fighting For More, Taking His Shot, Playing to Win (series collection)

Game of Love series

Rekindled, Captivated, Enamored, Game of Love (series box set)

Holiday Hearts series

Kiss Me Again, More Than Words, All I Want, Marry Me, Holiday Hearts (series box set)

Rocked by Love series

Love Notes, Love Song

The Philadelphia Frenzy series

Mad Scramble, Hometown Hero, Team Spirit

Bliss Bakery series

Sugar Crush, Heart of the Batter

The Falling series

Falling Faster

Other Novellas

Simmering Ice, Flirting on Ice, Iced (series box set) Tackled by the Girl Next Door

Sign up for Susan's reader newsletter, and never miss a new release:

https://www.susanscottshelley.com/newsletter